HAUNT

RACHEL H. DRAKE

ISBN-13: 978-1-959427-01-8 (Paperback)

ISBN-13: 978-1-959427-03-2 (Hardback)

ISBN-13: 978-1-959427-00-1 (Ebook)

Paperback Cover Designed by Alerim on 99Designs

Ebook and Hardback Cover Designed by Getpremades

Edited by Freedom Editorial

Interior Formatting by Rachel H. Drake

*For the wild part of me that wanted
to come out and play.*

TO HAVE, TO HAUNT

THE PLAYLIST

🎧 *Fuck Up the Friendship* - Leah Kate

🎧 *Pisces* - Miranda Glory

🎧 *cult leader* - KiNG MALA

🎧 *FU In My Head* - Cloudy June

🎧 *As the World Caves In* - Sarah Cothran

🎧 *Call Out My Name* - The Weeknd

🎧 *Hayloft* - Crypto, Jake Daniels

🎧 *Till Forever Falls Apart* - Ashe, FINNEAS

🎧 *Protection* - Peachkka

ABOUT THE SERIES: CREATURE CRAVINGS

The Creature Cravings series are interconnected standalone books. They can be read in any order, but are all set in the same world.

Each book features a unique paranormal couple and different tropes so you can satisfy the cravings in you. Find tropes organized for all currently available books in the series on rachelhdrake.com.

The author would love to hear from you! Record your reader reactions and share them with the author on Instagram by tagging @rachelhdrake.

CONTENT GUIDE

The Creature Cravings series is intended for mature audiences and features explicit sexual content.

Potential Triggers in Haunt:

- Mentions of the murder of a family, child included (not depicted)
- Depiction of using someone in a sexual ritual (consent is given for sex, but not the ritual)
- Mentions of narcissistic and emotional abuse in a family setting and two scenes of confronting the abuser (once verbally, once physically)

CHAPTER 1
HAUNTED

My ghost has always been with me.

The first memory I have of him was when I was six years old. I was hiding under my blanket, it was night, and my parents thought I was asleep. I could hear their yelling downstairs, like usual. My parents never mentioned it in the morning, but their arguments happened whenever Dad was home from his business trips, and I pretended I didn't hear them.

As I cried as softly as I could, I felt something brush my face. It was a soft caress, barely there and just for a moment. I didn't understand it then, but my body seemed to know I wasn't alone.

For years when I would cry, I would leave space in the center of my bed, and I would stare into that spot instead of the wall. My ghost comforted me and protected me so that I was never alone with my sadness. I can't see my ghost, there is no outline of a man or a shimmering in the corner of my eye. He is my invisible companion, using a cold breeze he commands to show me he is here.

Eventually, my Dad left and we stopped hearing from him. I think that is what hurt the most, that we weren't worth the trouble anymore. I don't see Mom much now that I'm an adult. I left the state on a college scholarship and never came back. We have become a holidays-only family.

But my ghost stayed with me, and is stronger now. It took some time, but now I feel a cold breeze in response to my feelings or questions daily. We've developed a language between us. Depending on where the breeze touches my body, I know what his answer is. If his breeze brushes my collarbone, the answer is yes. If he brushes my feet, the answer is no. While it is limited, I've learned a lot about him from simple yes or no answers.

He follows me into every room I am in. At first, he felt like protective big brother energy, but as I grew older, the energy became distinctly alluring. Sometimes I feel more for him than I can describe. He has kept me away from those who wanted to hurt me and has even comforted me when things didn't work out with my exes. Sometimes I feel his presence in the room when I shower or when I'm with another man, but I'm finding that I want him there too. There is something about his gaze that penetrates me. Even though I can't see him, I know exactly where he is looking.

Being haunted should scare me, but it never has. Like any other relationship, it grew with time. A deep-rooted part of me wants him and it seems like he does too, but I have been too scared to ask. I've been dreaming of him; a faceless man claiming me in the night. The dreams have happened so often, I've found myself waking up in a cold sweat reaching for my clit. I hold the vision of my dreams and touch myself, thinking of him and crying out.

What we have doesn't feel like enough anymore. I want to communicate with him in more than just yes or no answers, to hold his hand and feel his weight pressing into me at night. But he is a ghost, so that can't happen.

I exit my office and walk down the street. Work was frustrating today. Another client thought they knew better than the agency they hired to help them. I should be used to it by now, but it still gets to me. My ghost is behind me as I walk; a caress on my neck tells me so.

"I'm stressed," I complain aloud to him. The street

is empty, I had left a few minutes before the official 5:00 p.m. exit. The sidewalk has a distinct dirty and wet smell after the recent rainstorms that fits my mood.

My ghost responds with more pressure on my neck, sweeping my hair back with the breeze. There is a limit to how much he can touch me, but he knows how to use what is available to him. I shiver as the trail of his cold breeze runs down my arm.

"Have a good weekend, Emily!" my boss, George, calls from behind me as he leaves our favorite coffee shop. He turns back to the office after I wave my good-bye. George thankfully doesn't mind when I occasion-ally sneak out early. He trusts me to get the work done first. The people on our team are fairly nice and easy to get along with, but I've always been more of a loner. I've tried to make friends over the years, yet it never seems to work out. People don't seem to like being around me for long periods of time. Maybe I'm boring. The men that want to date me seem distinctly off, and the few I've actually dated over the years were fairly toxic. Having the occasional one-night stand when I had a need to be touched has been easier. I can take care of myself and I always have my ghost for company anyway.

I make it to my car and sit on the driver's side for a moment. My ghost continues to touch me and I feel the tension in my shoulders release. This year, there have been moments and touches that have lingered. A familiar thrumming starts between my legs. We haven't gone too far because how does that even start with a spiritual entity? What if I've misinterpreted what I've felt from him?

No, I tell myself. I'm sure I haven't. Even with the undead, attraction is hard to hide in close proximity.

There is also the question of who he was before he died. I never get far when I try to use our yes-and-no code to get answers on that. I know he is a man and older than me, but not his name or how he died. He hasn't wanted to answer any questions about his death.

"Thank you," I whisper when his ministrations still. I smile into the empty air like I'm used to. While I can't see him, I know he can see me, so I try to show I appreciate him however I can.

"Let's go home," I say and put my car into reverse. The weekend can not come soon enough.

THE THIRD GLASS OF WINE HAS SUFFICIENTLY LUBRICATED MY thoughts and inhibitions. While I do tend to have wine on Fridays, I don't usually get tipsy so quickly. I realize too late that I had skipped lunch and my quick dinner was not filling enough to keep me from getting accidentally drunk this evening.

I shut off the reality show I was watching with a click and toss the remote on my couch. My apartment is a mostly open-concept, the only separate space is my bedroom and bathroom. Most of the decorations are blue and green and I have fake plants everywhere. No real plants ever stayed alive long with me, no matter how closely I follow the instructions. I decided after a few years it was mean for me to keep trying only to kill them, so I switched to these dozens of fake IKEA plants.

When my thoughts start to whip across my brain at lightning speed, more wine begins to feel like a good idea. I am drowning in unrelenting frustration. I want to date a ghost, yet I can't even keep a plant alive. There is nothing I can do right. What has my life come to?

"I wish I could talk to you more," I call into the darkness of my living room. In this moment, I don't want to stop my thoughts. I want to say all the things I've kept to myself, fueled by liquid courage. There is the benefit that I don't have to stare at my ghost while I spill my thoughts. I can say it all without judging his body language or misunderstanding any hesitations.

"I wish I could touch you. Hold you. Hug you. I wish I knew for sure you also want that," I say and sniff, fingers tightening around the empty wine glass.

I feel the tears welling up in my brown eyes. His

breeze brushes my collarbone, answering yes to my yearning.

"I don't know how old you are, how you died, what you think. I know your *yes*, I know your *no*. But I can't hear you. I can't feel you deeply. I don't know when you are in pain."

I feel his breeze on my feet. What in my sentence was he saying *no* to?

"But you always know. You know when I'm scared, you know when I need help, when I'm sick, when I'm in pain. You know my joys." He has taken care of me in so many ways and I can barely talk to him. It isn't fair.

Another brush to my collarbone.

"But I don't know you," I whisper.

A brush to my feet. Does he think I do know him?

"I want to know you."

A brush to my collarbone in agreement and I feel the wine bring out the sadness in my heart and wring it out for my ghost to see.

After placing the wine glass back on the glass coffee table, I grab my phone and head for my bedroom. I strip naked as I walk, dropping my clothes as I go. Future Emily can clean the mess. I lie down in bed, curling under the blanket, my long brown hair spilling across my pillow

"I love you, Ghost. I want to feel you. I don't want to feel lonely when I'm with you." I sigh deeply, my eyes drawing closed without my permission. His cold presence joins me on the bed like every night.

With my last conscious thought, I make a wish, "I wish we could be together."

CHAPTER 2
FELT

Waking up to the sunrise is just a natural part of my day, even on the weekend and after drinking wine. My body has always held that rhythm, though there is usually more complaining after a night filled with wine. I pull myself out of bed and into the kitchen to get a glass of water. Most nights I put a glass of ice beside my bed so I have a cold drink when I wake up, but Past Emily didn't follow her routine.

I love living alone. Well, technically, I'm not alone with my ghost. But I didn't have a normal roommate, so starting and ending my days naked has become a common thing for me.

I frown into my glass and lean my chest against the cold counter with a groan. My pale skin pebbles with goosebumps. Ever since my ghost started using his breeze to touch me, I have been very receptive to anything cold. Everything I said last night is coming back to me and I'm not sure if I should be embarrassed or not for baring my soul to the undead.

Well, my ghost has seen me in some pretty compromising positions over the past few years of my adult life. It wasn't the first time he saw me drunk and naked and it wouldn't be the last. I chew on my lip. It will be fine. I'm sure he understands.

"I'm sorry about last night," I say into the morning air. My ghost replies with a brush to my feet. I hold my breath, needing to ask for clarification. This is the drawback of how we speak.

"Say *yes* if you mean I shouldn't be sorry and *no* if you mean you don't accept my apology."

He answers *yes*, lingering on my collarbone longer than necessary. I don't know if it is leftover wine in my system or just plain old courage, but I push the unwritten boundary we've set.

"I said I want to touch you. Do you want to touch me too?"

That same lingering touch answers. This is the boldest I have ever been with him. We have watched movies together and I have asked if he liked the plot. I told him that he was my best friend. I have thanked him for all the small ways he has shown me he was there. But I have never outright addressed the growing heat between us like I did just now. It seems so impossible that even saying it out loud feels like heartbreak. I wring my hands, barely able to hear my thoughts with how loud my heart is beating.

It's time to dive straight in; I can't keep going as I have. I don't know what I will do if he says no, but I have to try. My constant companion could say no and it would be weird between us until he finds someone else to haunt. Would he do that, move on to someone else? I brace myself. It's better to know for sure than assume.

"I meant sexually. Do you also want me that way?" I ask, recognizing that's a very vulnerable question when I'm already naked.

A swirling breeze sweeps past my collarbone and around my bare back before coming around to sweep between my breasts.

I can't control the slow smile spreading across my face. This is real—it's happening.

Okay, now what?

I steady myself, both hands gripping the kitchen island. My ghost's cold touch moves across my shoulders, to my breasts, and lower.

My arousal is immediate. His cold hasn't bothered me for years; that is how we speak to each other. When my feelings began to change, I started to add a few minutes of only cold water to my showers to feel closer to him. Eventually, a cold shower became part of my masturbation prelude.

"Okay," I start. "I'm going to lay down on my bed, and let's see what we can and can't do."

I practically run back to my bed, nearly sliding on the tile, one hand bracing my breasts. I take a deep breath and lie on top of the covers, unsure of what to do with my hands.

"I don't know what to do," I admit. "I'm so happy and nervous. Can you lead?"

His answer is clear as his cold caress snakes over me. I hum, nearly moaning as I sink deeper into my bed.

"I trust you," I say to him, knowing we are about to take a step I wouldn't have anticipated a few years ago. He applies a gentle pressure, but sparingly. He has never been able to touch me for long.

My hands grip my thighs as he seems to cover my body with prickling cold. My nipples rise and I feel myself growing damper. He asserts what pressure he is capable of on my right arm, traveling down and then touching my sensitive nub.

He repeats the movement and I arch into it. His touch is slight; a tease that he can't help.

"You want me to touch myself?" I pant, interpreting his message and already craving more. He responds with a *yes* and I listen, reaching to flick my clit. I apply pressure and close my eyes, imagining a faceless person taking over, doing what I desperately need him to do to me. His breeze peppers over me, focusing on where my hand is working, and I groan.

He adds bursts of cold to my clit in a rhythm as if he were my own supernatural vibrator. The feeling of his breeze used on my body with the distinct goal of my pleasure drives me wild. Every three seconds, another burst hits me, and I time my movements to fit in between his shivering pressures. I arc up with each burst, crying out as he teases me more and more.

I stop rubbing my clit and instead push my fingers one by one into me. My breathing grows heavier as I curl my fingers up to hit the spot I love so much. My legs widen and my ghost changes his pulsing cold to match the thrust of my fingers. In. Out. Curl. In. Out. Curl. Onward, I push myself until I'm whining, ready to come on my fingers.

"I'm almost there," I tell him and give myself more punishing thrusts, adding another finger.

I pump my hand faster, but eventually feel the steam leave me. Something is wrong. It's not enough. I crave more. The reality of him being here and not being able to touch me fully wears on me. He tries the pulsating again with his cold wind, but I have trouble reaching that initially tantalizing feeling.

I startle, pulled from my quest to come when my ghost uses his breeze to rattle the table beside my bed. I remove my hand. My ghost is asking to open a very particular drawer and I blush. He is always with me, so he knows what turns me on when I masturbate. Now he gets to take action on all he has observed and make it deliciously better.

I reach into the drawer and pull out a velvet-lined box. Lifting the lid, I see the glass dildo that I splurged on from that specialty sex shop. It's long, smooth, and see-through.

"I bought this thinking of you," I whisper, though I imagine he may have figured that out on his own. My hands are encouraged again but he helps mold my position to his liking. I straddle my bed, but before I can angle the dildo, my ghost covers my hand and my favorite tool in his cold. The glass absorbs his presence and I rub it along the slit of my folds until it's coated in my slickness. He follows my ministrations and then goes backward, swirling across my backside as I slowly push the dildo into my center.

I take a moment to realign my body before pushing it in and out, one hand controlling the cold glass and the other rubbing my clit. My knees push against the bedspread to give me purchase. I don't often do this position, but the more skin he can touch with his breeze, the better.

"I-I want you to touch my breasts," I request breathily as I shudder on the cold length of my substitute ghost dick.

He pushes on my breasts and for a moment I'm able to lean into what feels like a chest. I cry out, bucking against the dildo wildly at the thrill of connecting with him. I've never felt him like this before.

"My ghost," I call to him, grinding harder into my palm and leaning on him. I crash to the bed seconds later, the phantom chest no longer able to brace me. His cold surrounds me and I turn to lie on my back, giving my hand more access.

One hand pumps the dildo in, angling upward to hit me how I like. I can't stop the moans escaping me now, and I'm so grateful for the thick walls between me and my neighbors. Just knowing that he is here with me, participating and not just watching, makes it so much sexier.

"Touch. Me," I pant to my ghost, demanding more. He obliges how he can. I feel gentle pressure on my thighs; it's fleeting but it's there. I'm torn between lust and sadness, so thrilled to know he wants to be part of this, but upset that this is what we are dealt with. I pant, feeling sweaty and wounded, and wanting so much more. I've been close to coming, first with the pulsating cold and then as his breeze tickled the cold dildo, but stopping and starting and not being able to embrace him is getting in the way.

Spurred by my imagination, I describe what I have wanted him to do to me. I dare myself to say it aloud, to give him the gift of what fantasy we would have had.

"If you could touch me, I'd be bucking wildly beneath you right now. I'd pant your name. I'd cry out with each thrust. I'd thrill at you biting me. I'd ask for your come." I barely get the words out. My rubbing gets messier, hand no longer focusing on circles but rather on speed over my clit.

"I want to come on your dick so badly. I'd feel you filling me and that would be all I'd need to get off."

I shiver uncontrollably, closer and closer as I imagine what he would do. His phantom touches run along my neck and breasts, giving them attention as my hands stay occupied.

"I'd claw at your back," I say with a pant, adding as I crest over the precipice of my orgasm, "I'd scream. I'd be yours."

I moan as I clench onto the glass dildo, wishing it was his member made flesh.

My hips push upward and I feel his air hollow around my back and keep me upward, giving me a better angle.

"Yes, yes, yes," I call and feel a finger tickle between my legs that is not my own. It tips me over a new edge and I clench around the glass with a scream.

I fall back against my pillow, shivering and sweaty, the glass dildo abandoned in the middle of the bed. I have no energy to clean up yet. My ghost trails ice from my toes to my thighs and back, phantom fingers pressing at random intervals. *That* was new. I smile weakly into the cold of my pillow, momentarily sated.

I fall asleep with his presence beside me, and I know this is it. I need him and I need all of him. Nothing is going to stop me from raising the dead and having my way with him.

CHAPTER 3
THE CRYSTAL WITCH

When I woke a few hours later, I felt drained but pleased. It was still fairly early in the day, only eleven. I knew I had some errands to run today and other boring house things to do, but my thoughts were not capable of processing anything other than what we had just done. Consciously, I knew that my ghost had seen me masturbate and even watched me have sex with a few of my short-lived boyfriends, but never had he been part of that process. He'd never used what physical impact he could have on the world, his steady wind, in other ways.

Sometimes I wonder if I'm insane, that I cracked one day as a child and this is what I came up with. A ghost to love me that can never hurt me. Talk about abandonment issues. Is this a daddy complex, wanting love but never able to receive it from a male figure? Was I so desperate to have companionship I made it all up?

No. I can't be that damaged. If everyone with a shitty childhood was fucked up enough to imagine having a ghost lover, life would be really weird.

I stretch and get up from the bed, putting on my comfiest bra and leggings. I'll admit it is a struggle to get my leggings on. I feel more tired than I expected to be after such a long nap. Ghost sex is apparently more depleting than fucking a human.

He brushes my neck with his presence and I look over my shoulder. I have no clue if he is behind me or beside me, but I still say, "Hello," into the open space. "We're going to go out today."

I pull on my socks and then pad to my computer desk. Taking a seat, I turned on the monitor and opened up Google like any other millennial would do. This isn't the first time I have explored ghosts in my Google searches, and it probably isn't even the hundredth time, but after what happened yesterday I'm not going to give up until I have answers. Not a lot has made sense in my previous searches since none of the first-hand accounts of ghost experiences are even close to what was real to me.

Firstly, I can't see my ghost, but I can feel his presence. He doesn't talk to me with a voice or focus on scaring me like in other recorded accounts. Secondly, my ghost has always been calm and has communicated with me through his breeze. Communicating with concentrated wind seems to be the most unique part from what I've seen. The only other power he has that I know about is that sometimes he can add more force to the breeze and it feels like a physical touch. I thought I felt his fingers for a brief moment, but that can't be right. He has never done that before, but I've also never invited him into my bed. Well, that's not true. We sleep together all the time, but not in *that* way.

This is not a normal ghost story. There is something different about him. Either that or every other account I have read is wrong. Or maybe each ghost experience is supposed to be unique? I hate all this back and forth. I hang my head in my hands. If only there was a manual on this sort of thing.

I have to take this further and get professional help. A séance or some sort of reading seems like the next step. Not to stop these events from happening again, because that isn't what I want. But being able to talk to him? To know how he died? I will do anything to just be in his life more and to have him in mine. Does it make me selfish to not want him to move on? Does he want to move on in the first place? It seems irresponsible of me that I haven't even wondered that until now.

Using an online psychic feels too impersonal. Plus,

I won't be able to watch and see if they are pulling up dictionaries on Tarot meanings or using other means to make a fake reading. This life with my ghost is real to me and I am finally ready for answers. I want to be in a room with my ghost, the psychic, and me to get this reading so I'll know if they are being true to my experience.

I open Google Maps and look for psychics near me. I sort through close ones and read their reviews. Some of the reviews are obviously fake or way too enthusiastic, so I cross those locations off my list. Eventually, I decide on The Crystal Witch, a location only ten miles away from my apartment.

I'm surprised there are so many physical psychic locations close to me. Apparently, there is a whole section of the city called Witchy Playground—according to a Redditor—where there are several blocks of shops and centers close to each other for psychics, witches, and other magical needs. If The Crystal Witch ends up not being the real deal, at least I have options on that strip.

I get up from my computer, throw on my long cream knit sweater, braid my hair in a French braid, and put on my sneakers.

"Ghost?" I call into my apartment. I feel an immediate chill and know he is listening. Living with a ghost has saved a lot on my AC bill.

"We are going to a psychic. I want to talk to you,

get some ideas on what I can do to help you, and a psychic may be able to help. Please stay close to me, okay?"

The chill brushes my neck and I smile. "Let's go."

THE DRIVE TO THE CRYSTAL WITCH WAS SHORT. I PARK ON the street in a rare moment of perfect parallel parking, patting myself on the back before I step out of my car. The street matches the Witchy Playground look I was expecting; lots of dark purples and greens, signs with pentagrams, crystals, and plants. There's a store that claims to be the Home Depot plant department, but for witchy plants only, which seems like smart marketing. A few people go in and out of their shop as I watch. Too bad I'd probably kill the plants just by being in their presence.

I find The Crystal Witch and open the door, jumping at the automatic bell that plays. The cashier greets me with a nod, but otherwise ignores me and gets back to reading her book.

"Make yourself at home! I'll be right out," a voice says from one of the back rooms.

Lining the walls are books for sale. I make a mental note to look at them should the reading go well. There are other tables of items available, like tarot cards and crystals of all sizes and colors. I recognize a few of the crystals by name from random social media ads, like the gorgeous selenite lamp, or the rose quartz for romance, but most are a mystery. Overall, the store feels homey and welcoming with several areas for seating and a couch off to the left. A sign reads "Join our Wiccan book club!" in a bold font with a pentagram replacing the period in the exclamation point.

"Hi, I'm Rosie, the witch and psychic behind this establishment. It's a pleasure to meet you."

I turn around to see a tall, pink haired tan woman draped in a black fitted satin dress. On her neck is a pink crystal heart pendant as bright as her hair. Her lips are thin and painted brown, and she welcomes me with a wide smile and sparkling green eyes.

"Hi," I reply breathlessly, overcome with nerves. So much relies on this conversation. "I'm Emily."

"How can I help you today, Emily?" Rosie asks. Her eyes glaze over slightly, looking above and to the left of my head.

I turn around, expecting to see someone else coming through the door but the space behind me is empty.

"I'm looking for a reading," I say. "Are you available now or do I need to make an appointment?"

"Of course, I'd be happy to help you right now." She looks behind me for a second, holding onto her pendant, fingering the stone. Can she see my ghost? "Have you already reviewed our packages online?"

"Yes, I'd like the communication package," I say. It seems like the safest place to start. It detailed a thirty-minute reading where a psychic will help you reach a spirit of your choosing across any supposed plane and share what messages they want to bring to you. That is, as long as the spirit wants to talk to you, the convenient asterisk detailed. I wonder how often Rosie needed to use the asterisk clause.

"Great," Rosie says. "Follow me to our private room."

She leads me to the back corner where a solo black door stands between two bookshelves. I can't help but speed read a few titles as she opens the door, finding rather interesting topics like *Raising Your Children Witchy* and *How to Read Auras*.

"So, I imagine you would like to communicate with the ghost that came in with you today," Rosie comments as she ushers me in. I feel an immediate sense of relief, knowing I made the right decision to come here and have found legitimate help.

"Yes, this ghost has been my friend for many years, but something has changed recently so I'd like to talk with him more." It feels so nice to talk about my ghost, to say the words aloud I have never said before.

"I would love to assist you. Thank you for coming to The Crystal Witch," Rosie says.

She gestures to a black-covered table and chairs lined with glittering stars. In the center stands a large smoky quartz crystal instead of the usual crystal balls I have seen on TV. The room is darker than the rest of the store with only an amber bulb lit in the room and a few scattered candles. The window is covered with a blackout curtain.

"Sit and we'll feel the energy surrounding your aura." We sit across from each other in the low-lit room, shadows playing across her face.

I swallow, curious and a little scared. Best case scenario, I will know my ghost. Worst case, I will have no new information.

"Now there are a few things I like to do in these readings," Rosie explains. "They may seem simple, but often I find that the more complicated we make communicating with the dead, the less accurate the result is. There are many beings that want to talk to us and all they need is a receptive ear, like me, to speak. Those that need to be brought through with long gate-keeping rituals are often not those that my guests actually needed, but rather something forced."

"That makes sense," I comment, though I'm not really sure. How can this be easy?

"First, I'm going to simply ask the room and see what I feel. We might get a message or we might not. Sometimes it's simply transmitted feelings, pictures, and rarely exact words. Spirits aren't always able to talk the way we do, or if they do, it's on a wavelength that is harder to interpret so we see visual representations. Then we'll work with tarot cards to bring about other messages tied to this being. Okay? Any questions?"

"No questions," I say.

Rosie takes both of my hands in hers, forming a circle around the smoky quartz. I shift in my seat, nervous all of a sudden.

"Deep breaths, Emily," she requests.

Together we breathe in and out for a few beats, and Rosie's eyes close.

She speaks into the dim light, "Does anyone or anything need to speak to Emily today?"

I shiver, the chill of my ghost dusting my shoulders. Rosie seems to feel it too and smiles to herself, eyes still closed.

"Hello, Spirit. What do you have to say to Emily?"

There is a pause and Rosie's head tilts as if listening.

"Is my ghost talking?" I whisper after a few seconds, giddy and impatient.

"This being feels as familiar with you as you do with it," Rosie says. "He also says you are his. But he is not a ghost, not exactly."

"What?" I sputter, hands gripping hers tighter. A light breeze circles the room and Rosie opens her eyes. She isn't smiling now.

"Let's consult the cards."

I pull my hands back. "What do you mean? What did he say?"

"It was a feeling, not exact words. The spirit didn't feel dead like a true ghost. It is something living and dead at the same time. It feels possessive of you. I have felt something similar before, but not in an incorporeal being. And you, too, feel different. There an aspect in your aura not recognized by your full self yet. Now that I'm aware of it..." She pauses and looks at me, her eyes roaming over my face and the space behind me. "I can sense how it is latched to you. The spirit holds onto you like a tether. Let's learn more, Emily, so you can make an informed decision."

Rosie takes her pink hair into a bun. It unnerves me, as if my psychic has to prepare herself for something.

"What decision would I need to make?" I ask, stroking my arms.

"Whether or not you want this being to continue to have a claim on you," Rosie explains patiently.

The answer has always been, and will continue to be, *yes*.

CHAPTER 4
CLAIM

Rosie takes a deck from the shelf behind her and shuffles. "Tell me about the spirit you call your ghost while I shuffle."

"I don't even know where I'd start," I say. There is no simple way to explain the presence that has enriched my life for decades.

"Start at the beginning. When were you first contacted?"

"He has always been there. I didn't feel the shivers or coldness grow bolder until recent years, but when I was younger I always felt like I was watched. It didn't feel evil. It was a calming presence, and I'd feel it stronger when I was sad or angry. Sometimes when I wake up, I think I hear a whisper of my name but it fades quickly. We have found a way to answer yes and no questions together, but I want to communicate more directly."

Rosie hums as she continues to shuffle. A few cards pop out and she puts them to the side, face down. "Why do you want to communicate differently with him now?"

"I feel more urgency from him. We've started to connect more, I guess you could say. I want to talk with him and learn why. Why me and how can I help him?"

"Help him to leave?" Rosie asks, seeking clarification.

My heart clenches and I hesitate to answer.

"You can trust me, Emily," Rosie assures me, squeezing my hand.

"No, I don't want him to move on, not unless that is what he wants. I want to keep him." I tell her the truth because if anyone can help me it was this witch.

"What changed in your life that could have impacted the spirit?" Rosie asks.

I came to get answers, so as sensitive as this topic is, I have to tell her.

"We have started a sexual relationship," I admit, heart beating quickly.

She nods as if it doesn't shock her. Maybe it doesn't, she must see a lot in her line of work.

Rosie puts the deck down and cuts it into three piles.

She overturns the first card in each pile and calls them out, "This represents the past." She holds up the first card, The Devil. "The present." She points at the middle card, The Sun. "And the future." The final card is listed as The Fool.

Without knowing what the tarot cards' meanings are by heart, I feel uneasy.

Rosie taps her lips as she focuses on the cards, then begins to explain, "The Devil is not as dire a card as it seems, but there is a lesson with it that can point to a negative outcome if the warning is not headed." Rosie pushes the card toward me, turning it around so I can look closely. The Devil is shown as a half-goat, half-human hybrid with wings and an inverted pentagram on its forehead. "The Devil card is telling you that there is an attachment holding you back. In the past position, it could be a memory or experience, or a negative force from the past still exerting its power on you. What thought comes to your mind when I say that?"

"My dad leaving me," I say immediately, then blink. My ghost tells me *yes* with his breeze. He agrees, but why?

"I don't know why I said that," I admit in a whisper, laying a hand on my heart.

Rosie's eyes follow the movement and she comments, "Something in you had you speak of him, so he is a key to that attachment that is hurting you. Think on that as we continue our reading."

She turns the middle card to me, a shining sun staring happily back at me. "The Sun is a positive sign, especially when in the present position and upright. The Sun is warming comfort and a happy influence in your life. This may be your current relationship with your ghost. But when you stay in the sun, you can burn, so see this as a transitional card on the way to something new." She taps the card to emphasize the point and turns to the next one. "In the future, we have The Fool. Despite its name, this does not mean you will make a mistake or a fool of yourself. The Fool is the start of a new adventure should you accept it. You do still need caution, as with most things, but you are here. You listen to your guides. I don't think you will choose the wrong path."

Rosie picks up the deck again. "Let's ask about this change and see if there is more guidance for you." She shuffles with her eyes closed. As she does, a card pops out and lands sideways, neither upright or reversed. She opens one eye, sniffs as if flustered, then shuffles again. She adds a few cards to a separate pile before turning back to what popped out.

Picking up the card, she reveals it to me as The Tower. She leaves it in this medium position, letting it lay as it fell. I focus on the illustration on the card, people jumping out of a fiery building. I feel a drop in the pit of my stomach and the air in the room seems to thin.

"You will be faced with significant life changes if you decide to continue with this spirit," Rosie warns. "The Tower often symbolizes a fork in the road. There is an option being presented to you soon that will be this change and will solidify your path."

She holds her right hand over the card, her left reaching in and choosing a crystal from a dish. She focuses on the crystal and the card and says, "This decision will be irreversible. Once you reach it, you'll know it is a defining one."

Rosie looks through the other cards that popped out of the deck and puts them aside.

"What did those say?" I ask. Did they say something horrible? Why would she hide them?

"Nothing for you, Emily. Don't worry," she says, seeming to pick up on my nerves. "My guides were telling me I would have more visitors like you that need help with spiritual and other worldly relationships."

"So there are more spirits like my ghost?" I ask, hopeful that this would mean I could get more answers.

"No." Rosie shakes her head. She grasps her crystal heart necklace, her thumb rubbing back and forth over the pendant. "What is your ultimate goal? What do you want to accomplish with your ghost?"

"I want to talk to him, firstly," I say and then take a deep breath before adding, "I want to date him, be able to see him. I want him resurrected, or alive again, or just visible and touchable. I don't know what my options are."

"That's a lofty goal," Rosie says with a chuckle, but not judgment. She turns back to the large crystal in the center of the table and takes another few deep breaths like she did at the start of our session. "If you want him to join you in the 3D realm, it is tied to that defining moment. He will know what to do. And it is tied to the physical part of your relationship. That is what I'm feeling when I think about how his spirit feels alive and dead simultaneously. There is a tie to your mutual attraction and something from your past." She points to the devil card.

My heart sings. I have confirmation that I can keep him, that he can be brought back to life.

"How will I know though, if he can't talk to me?" I ask.

She lets go of the necklace and smiles at me. "This is a communication reading and I will help you call that in. As I said, there is something unique about this relationship. You are a creator here, bringing him forth with sexual energy. The more that physical side of your relationship grows, the stronger he will be. I'm sure there is a tie to sex and his expression. Alive, but dead. The rules are different here."

She pauses for a moment, then asks with a slow drawl, "Do you feel drained after engaging with him?"

"Yes, we've only been together once. This morning. But I slept for hours afterward."

Damn, I admit to myself. This psychic is good. Score one for Google and Reddit. How did she know to ask that?

"Then yes, it is that tie," Rosie confirms. "You have to pace yourself. He needs your feminine creation energy and that means taking it from you. You will rebuild that energy in your sleep, but you shouldn't expel too much at a time. If you can, I would suggest no more than three days a week so that you aren't endangered in this process."

"So there is hope that he could join me as a human with time?" My hopes have doubled since entering this room.

"He'll never be human, but he could be corporeal. I have a suggested ritual for you, but it is a very personal and intimate one given how he gathers strength. Would you be open to trying it with me?" Rosie stands from the table and adjusts her skirt, glancing at me and the space behind my shoulder.

"Yes," I say without hesitation. "Anything to speak with him. What do I have to do?"

CHAPTER 5

INTENTIONS

R osie comes back into the room with an arm full of supplies. She drops them into the center of the table and asks me to move to the side. I do so and watch as she pushes our chairs and the table off to the right of the room. She takes the blanket she brought with her and gives it a fluff before laying it on the floor in the center of the room, then places candles around it.

"I'm going to set these up and then explain their purpose. You don't have to use everything I set up. Follow your intuition and cues from your ghost," Rosie tells me as she busies herself. She points to sections around the elaborate setup and explains each. "Candles in red for passion, blue for healing, and black for protection. They are arranged to a point for a transformation triangle."

In the middle of the triangle, on the blanket, is a black smooth crystal that is distinctively phallic. It stands upright with a flat base to keep it from laying on the floor.

"That," she says, "is a black tourmaline crystal. It will help you detox from previous sexual encounters and partners if used internally and make way for new positive experiences. Use this crystal in any way that makes sense to you."

The sly look on Rosie's face tells me the stone is indeed phallic shaped on purpose. I swallow nervously.

"I am an observer in this situation," Rosie continues. "I have given you what can help bring you both together, but since this is your own stamp on the magic, whatever you need and however you want to use it is up to you."

She takes one more glance around, sharing a few more points of interest on the crystals, and what incense was chosen and why, before circling the space and chanting. She says something about a safe circle and inviting only the spirit I choose, but I tune it out. She is talking to the room, not me. My ghost is distracting me, caressing my neck, and I find myself leaning against the wall as if it is him.

Rosie stops her chanting and steps in my line of vision, calling my attention back. "Take off your clothes and sit in the center of the circle. Say what you want to accomplish with your ghost, and the tools around you will help hone that energy, Emily. Touch yourself while delivering your intention."

"What?" I sputter, shocked despite her earlier insinuation. The temperature in the room grows colder. Rosie turns off the amber lamp, leaving only the glow of the candles. The room is devoid of most light except for the center triangle.

"He is connected through your creation energy. Use that here. This is a safe space. I will stand in a corner to observe, should you need any guidance. You don't need to *complete* what you start right now, but edge yourself close to orgasm so that your divine energy is combined with your intention."

The caress on my neck reaches down and across, grabbing my right breast. Rosie raises an eyebrow, looking down at the disturbed fabric. "He thinks it's a good idea," she encourages. She hands me a glass container of ceremonial rose oil and gestures to the triangle.

I nod and swallow, realizing I'm about to *perform* in front of a witch. The phantom hand touches the small of my back in encouragement. Rosie is right—he is stronger through our sexual encounters. Even in the few hours from this morning, he is more forward and able to give more of his touch to me. What she has set up will work.

I came to her for answers, I can't get nervous and back out now that she has given them to me.

I slowly take off my clothes and fold them, leaving them in a pile next to Rosie and enter the circle. Settling on my knees in the center, I add a dab of the oil to my hands.

"Tell him what you want," she reminds me.

"My ghost?" I call.

The candle flames flickers in answer.

I glance nervously at Rosie, my hands reaching between my thighs. She gives a reassuring smile. "You are safe with me, Emily. I am here to help facilitate what you want."

I smile gratefully back and refocus. Gazing at the center black crystal, I dip my index finger between my folds, sliding up and down.

"Ghost," I say again. "I want to talk to you."

He tickles my chest. I gasp, my small breasts heaving up and down as my breath quickens.

"It's important to me that we speak with words, if you are able to. I want to know you. If not words, another way where we can speak further than yes and no. Help me communicate with you." I whisper the words, occasionally pausing as I stroke. "I want you to be with me, physically, daily. When we talk, tell me how to help you. Tell me what to do to bring you forth with me."

I begin slow circles on my clit, feeling a familiar

anticipation course through me. A moan escapes me. My ghost hovers somewhere in front of me and I rub the circles faster. My breasts spill forward as one of my hands braces on the floor and I lean down. His strengthened hands caress me, reaching for my clit.

I'm shaking now, no longer thinking of Rosie in the corner or the fact that I was in a triangle of candles.

"I want to see you. I want to hear you. I want to be with you. I'm calling you to me now. Use what I'm giving you." I moan the words, losing myself.

My legs shake as I approach my release. I accidentally brush near the standing crystal and my body shudders. I inch forward without thought, rubbing myself on the long length of the crystal. Ghost steps in, covering the crystal with his freezing wind. When the tower of wind releases it, the crystal is as cold as his presence.

I keen for my ghost, releasing my clit and pulling myself back up. I plunge myself onto the crystal, grateful for its blunted shape, and groan. I pump up and down, pretending it is the object of my desires, my ghost.

The fire around me rises up in skinny columns, flickering. I distantly hear a gasp behind me, but pay no mind.

I speak to my ghost about the life we'd have, the children I'd want if we could. I describe how wondrous it would feel to be in his arms. I describe what our family would be like and how it would feel so different from the crying nights we spent together when I was a child. I talk at great length about our sex life, the positions I wanted to try, and how good his come would feel between my legs. I don't stop talking, not until my body is shaking and the fire begins to calm in both me and the candles.

I shatter, released from the sexual trance, and I whisper my final intention, "Come alive for me. Be here. Use your voice to tell me how." His wind tells me *yes, yes, yes* as I plead, "Make love to me."

When I calm down and feel the compulsive need release me, the mortification sets in. Had I just fucked a crystal dick in front of a psychic witch? My face heats and I lift myself off of the crystal. I turn to look at Rosie. The crystal is slick with my juices and Rosie eyes it.

"Well," Rosie says and fans her face. "Good job. Also..." She moves away from the corner and points to the dildo. "That's our new standing crystal dildo line. I would love it if you'd leave a review of it on our website. We've done some product testing, but it's new to the store. I'm glad you liked it so much. It looks like it accomplished what I hoped, helping you release the pain of your childhood and family life."

I bark a laugh, feeling less self-conscious now that she went for a marketing angle and combined it with the reading. "You are good at this, Rosie."

"Yes, I am," she says with her own low laugh.

She ushers me to the bathroom to clean up and get dressed. When I return, most of the set up is cleared. She hands me a bag and I glance inside to see the crystal dildo has been cleaned and packed for me. I spot some other candles and a book on simple spells, auras, and the magic of color theory. I smile gratefully for the gift, but my chest does heat with a blush.

"Do you think it worked?" I ask her.

"The air was impregnated with your magic and intention. I think it will work. Rest tonight, go to sleep to replenish your energy, and see what has changed by the time you wake up."

"Thank you, Rosie. I'll try that. Does he have a message for me right now? Is he asking or showing you anything else before I go?" I'm hopeful; desperate that this ceremony worked. I certainly got more than I bargained for with the communication package.

"He is radiating love. He shares your feelings, Emily," Rosie tells me.

I smile in the dark, hoping to hear what he thinks from his own mouth by morning.

I pay at the register, being sure to add a substantial tip. With how the cashier is staring me down, I wonder how soundproof the room was.

I walk quickly toward the door and Rosie calls after me, "I expect to hear how it all went in a few days!"

CHAPTER 6
TO WANT

Going to sleep was difficult last night, but I practiced what I've seen on online about holding your intention and focused on how good it would feel to be able to talk to him. I thought about what Rosie said about my aura and its unrecognized parts. What does that mean? I ruminated on it and whether or not the sex ritual worked for hours. I didn't feel much of my ghost last night and it worries me. I hope that's a good sign rather than the opposite and his silence was what he needs to reclaim his voice. Or for all I know, he's asleep too. Do ghosts sleep?

I sit up quickly as I wake, looking around with wide eyes.

"Ghost?" I call into the quiet apartment. It has been years since I've slept in this late. My body feels like I ran a marathon despite the long hours of sleep, but my mind? It's more awake than ever.

I'm here, my Emily. I was waiting for you. My name is William.

I gasp. The voice reverberates in my mind, as clear as my own thoughts but distinctly male. His voice is deep and echoing.

It's me, he says before I can reply. As if it would be anyone else.

"I'm so glad to hear you. Hi, William," I say, a lone tear falling down my cheek. His cold wind tickles my face as if to wipe it away. "Are you really here?" I can't help but ask. After wishing for this for so long, I'm scared and simultaneously happy.

I'm here, my angel.

"You are the ghost, not me. You should be *my* angel." I fall back on my pillow and smile toward the other half of my bed. I reach to the empty side and slide through cold air. My skin goosebumps and I rearrange myself comfortably under the covers, my black silk slip moving up my thighs. It has been so stressful thinking about what could go wrong that I put on my most expensive pajamas just to feel better.

You are my angel. You are bringing me back to life. You are a miracle.

"Really? I can save you?" I ask in a higher pitch than usual, not used to being complimented and ecstatic in knowing it was possible to have what we both want.

Yes. Yes. I'm so glad to speak with you and have you hear me. His voice is so warm in my head, so real and crisp, like a hug on my heart. I'm used to thinking of him as cold, and while it is a welcome coldness, it's different to feel the warmth of love and hope blossom in me.

"What should we talk about first?" I ask. The world is so big, so open, and it's as if we are old friends and new acquaintances at the same time.

Everything. Everything we've both wanted to ask or say.

"I've always wanted to talk to you. To know for sure I was not imagining things." My voice breaks. It was going to be an emotional day. I decide to call George later and tell him I'm sick and need a few days off. I can talk to my ghost and be with him, finally, and nothing will get in the way of that.

I've always been yours. I've always been with you, his velvety voice tells me.

"My first memory of you is when I was six. Is that when you first came to me? Or was it before then and I was too young to remember? How did you get to be with me?" I have so much I want to know.

That's right. That was when we first met.

"How did you die? How did you find me?"

I was murdered, me and my family. After my death, I

woke up and I was with you. You were crying so I decided to stay. I remember not wanting to see you sad.

"I'm so sorry William. Do you remember it? The person who did this to you?" To think that someone hurt him, that his death was not a natural one or an accident, breaks my chest in half.

No, I remember before it happened. I remember my life. I remember the feeling of death and that life was taken from me. I felt the pain of my murder and the sadness as I watched my parents die, but not who. It's blocked from me.

"Are your parents ghosts too?" I whisper.

No, I don't think they are ghosts. At least, if they are, I haven't seen them.

"That sounds so lonely." I hug myself since I am unable to hug him.

I have felt loneliness, but not because I'm the only ghost I know.

"Then why?" I ask, hoping I can fix it. He has always helped me feel less alone and if I can return the favor, I will.

Because I couldn't talk to you. I know we would talk through yes or no questions, I'm glad we had that, but it wasn't the same.

"That made me feel lonely too. I always felt you, but even when you were there, I felt like I was in an empty room, and you were behind a wall."

I don't want that Emily. I don't want to feel like an empty room.

"I'm sorry, William. Do you know why Rosie said you were both alive and dead? What does that mean?"

I am aging. Even as a ghost, my mind, my ghost body, it's growing older with you.

"How old are you?" I've always wondered this question, and he would never give me a straight answer. Even when I'd go up a scale of numbers and ask him yes or no, he couldn't answer. This must be why. Ghosts shouldn't age, but he was.

I'm 32, I was 11 when I died.

"What did you mean when you said your ghost body changed?"

I can see my body, even though you can't.

"What do you look like?" I find myself wondering how ghosts get clothes. If he is getting older, did he grow out of the clothes he was wearing when he died or did it evolve with him? Is he naked? Can he imagine whatever he wants to wear?

Let's keep that a surprise for when you bring me back. If you agree to it.

"Of course I'll agree to it," I say, offended that he doubts that. I frown at the empty space on my bed. "How do I do it?"

Do you care about me, Emily? he asks instead.

"Of course I do."

Do you want to be in a relationship with me?

"Yes," I hedge, "I thought that might be obvious with what we've done."

For what we'd need to do, you have to be sure. You have to want it all, like me. I know what you said yesterday, about our family and who we could be. I feel that, too. I want to possess you, keep you, hold you. But you don't know everything yet. You might change your mind.

"I've trusted you for years, William. You've proven yourself to me. Nothing you have to tell me will change that," I say with a promise. While I mean it, I'm also holding my breath. What does he think is so bad that I won't want to save him?

I feel so alive when we touch. I feel stronger. What Rosie alluded to was true. I can feed on our energy when we are intimate. It is the nature of who I am. Before I died, I was from a family of succubi demons. Even as a ghost, I still maintain the powers of an incubus, a male succubus. I hadn't reached maturity yet when I died, my powers hadn't manifested, but part of me was still drawn to certain energies. I am sure that is what kept me on this plane, not dead but not alive. I've felt my needs manifest in me as I've grown up with you. It took longer, without a body, but I feel it now. I choose you.

"Succubi are real?" I ask the question I need to ask, but his last sentence is sparkling in my mind. Knowing he chose me is the only heaven I need.

Yes, my Emily. I've chosen you. If I feed more on you, I can come back. You kept my soul alive, and with your body I can be reborn.

I don't know what I expected when I decided to go

on this journey with my ghost, but learning about succubi and incubi was not one of them. But am I surprised? Yes. Does it startle me? Not as much as I thought. Though if sex demons are real, what else is out there?

"Tell me more," I say, though my body is already thrumming with anticipation. "What does it mean to be an incubus and what would it mean for me if I was with you?"

Pleasure. Safety. Trust. Promise. Possession. It means I'll worship you. It's not the same for every couple in this kind of relationship, but for me that's what I want. I've been dead and bodiless for years, you would be my first, and I want you to be my only. To be an incubus, you feed on sexual energy and on the creation of life. It makes you stronger, gives you more energy, it makes you whole. We can live without it, but something is always missing. When you feed on someone, they grow more tired. There is a point where you can take too much.

"When I masturbated before and you participated, and then at The Crystal Witch, did you feed on me?"

Yes. Part of it was subconscious. I wasn't aware I was at first, but I felt different afterwards. Stronger. It's how I can talk to you now. What you did with Rosie worked because it combined that creation and passionate energy together when combined with her tools and your intention.

"So how long I slept last night, and the nap earlier

in the day, was because I was fed on?" My new sleeping habits made more sense now.

Yes, it temporarily takes from you and, depending on the drain, you'll be fine in a few hours most of the time.

That didn't seem too bad. If sleeping in was the worst side effect, sign me up.

"I love you, William. Without knowing it all, I know that I love you and this doesn't scare me away. There is more for us to do together. I know I'll have more to ask you and so much to learn about what this means, but none of that will change my feelings."

I love you too, my Emily.

"I want to feed you again," I say breathily, rubbing my thighs together. "I want to give you what you need so that you can grow stronger and stay with me."

I am dying to eat you, my love.

CHAPTER 7
TO BE TOUCHED

My ghost is an incubus. It all makes sense. Anticipation—a drunk anticipation—is coursing through me. He is alive and dead. He's been growing with me, attached to me, a ghost even more paranormal than the usual kind, feeding on me.

And loving me.

Emily. Emily, his voice moans my name. *Remove your clothes.*

I listen to my ghost and remove the satin slip I had slept in. His presence is closer, a coldness to the air that puckers my nipples. My body is shaking as I remove my underwear. These seconds of waiting are painful, hurting, a barrier between our needs. I've wanted him for so long. To talk to him, hold him, touch him, fuck him, and now he's here.

Yes, like that Emily. Think of me. Call me in.

He senses my thoughts, my need for him, and has asked for more. I oblige, smiling and stretching across my bed like a satisfied cat. My inner thighs feel sore from pounding the crystal yesterday. Just like that ritual, I feel a wild compulsion. Now that I know who and what he is, I expect it—thrive in it. I want him to use me. I want to give myself to him and in return, get to keep him.

"I want you, my ghost," I say to him. My William. After so many years where he could not speak to me, he became my ghost, even though we have spent the last thirty minutes talking and speaking his new name. I think he prefers being my ghost, to be called by the inaccurate spirit name, the only one I could think of when I first became aware of him.

I am here, my angel, he says into my mind, and I swear there is breath on my neck. I shiver.

"What do I do?" I ask my spirit. My hands float along my face and lips, wishing he were kissing me.

Let me touch you. I yearn to touch you.

"I want to touch you and for you to touch me. How much do you need to feed to do that? How much to come alive fully?" As I speak, I lay back on the bed, legs spread wide with want. I've never been so forward, practically wanton with my need to be fucked. The weeks of sex dreams were fueled by him, my dramatic increase in how often I masturbated, the events of yesterday with our mutual sexual discovery and the ritual at The Crystal Witch, it all had been for him, with him, to bring me here.

Imagine me touching you. Feel me touching you. My hand is here, worshiping your breast. Make me stronger, Emily, and I'll touch you. Feed me.

I feel a slick of cold cross my chest and my cunt floods. This is real. Nothing has ever felt more real and important to me.

"I felt it. I feel you," I call into my ceiling. There is a building in me, something uncontrollable in my cells. I run my hands along my stomach and to my pussy, gently caressing.

My good girl. My Emily, my ghost tells me and I practically purr at the praise.

"Yes, I'm your Emily. Please touch your Emily."

I feel him pulsing near and there is a delicious tug deep in me. My legs spread impossibly wider and I groan, knowing keenly that he is on me, doing all he can to feel me. It's nearly there. Whatever is happening, it's working.

"Keep going. Keep trying. How? How can I help you?"

Your energy, Emily. You are giving it to me. Feeding me, giving me life. You taste so good, Emily.

A phantom tongue grazes my clit and I punt up, hoping to feel resistance, but it goes through muddy thick air. Slowed, but not a form, and I want to cry. He is so close, but so far away.

"Come to me, come to me, feed on me," I pant, needing more and left wanting as I gyrate to the thickened air before me. He is here. He is with me.

I know what to do now, Emily. I know how we can be together. I have a plan.

"How? Tell me and I will do it." I'm desperate. I've already done sex magic, there's no harm in doing more.

Bring someone else to our bed. Bring someone else here for me to feed on. A substitute for me until I can be here.

"Someone to murder?" What in the world has my life come to that this is what I'm contemplating right now? I pause my ministrations, not able to get off at the thought of death despite sleeping with a ghost.

No, I would never ask you to kill someone, Emily. Bring someone, someone that needs you. Needs your body. Bring them here, touch them, use them, and I'll take what I need. Someone that is desperate for you. The more he wants you, the more I can feed on him and the stronger I will become.

"You want me to be with someone else?" A pang stabs my chest, sharp and threatening. I am happy for him to use me, feed on me, but only if we are to be together. If he doesn't truly care for me, and sees me only as an opportunity to be in my world, I don't think I can do this. It's selfish, I know, but he was made for me. I cannot see him in this world with anyone else.

Never. You are mine, Emily. But I need more energy than I can safely take from you. I need that energy building and I can't do that yet. When this person touches you, and touches you fully, it will feed me. I will touch you in my own way, as I can. I will be here loving you, taking in your pleasure, and then we can be together. If I take more from you, I'll hurt you. We need someone else to bolster the energy. Trust me, my baby, my Emily. Let me love you. Find someone—someone needy. Bring them here now. While I am strong in this moment, I can get stronger. It has to be now. If we do this, I can have a body again. You will be able to see me, feel me, and keep me. Once this is done, you don't ever have to have someone else in your bed, not unless you want to.

The wet cold of his presence pulls on my gut. A weight surrounds me full of love and longing. It breaks me open, turns me on, and I know now I never had a chance. My fears are short lived and wrong. He wants me, but he needs more sexual energy than my body is capable of on my own. Not *yet*, anyway. Knowing this, I retract my earlier thoughts. I will do whatever William asks to be claimed by him. I will kill if I have to. He has always protected me, and I'll now protect him.

I think on what he has told me about being an incubus. How they feed on intention, energy, passion, and sex. I was exhausted after our first intimate time together and even more so when I worked with Rosie to give him a voice. He took my energy to do these limited things. Even those nights when I woke up and masturbated from dreams of him, I see now was also a craving for his incubus nature, and I was drained then, too. I need someone that is willing to be with me, desperate for me as William said, just for the night. No mere ex-boyfriend will do.

I know exactly who will have the most energy for him to feed on. William may not like me choosing this person. In fact, he'll hate it. He warned me to stay away from him in his own way with our unspoken language last year. He was right; this person is not trustworthy. Not in the slightest.

He will be perfect for William to feed on.

CHAPTER 8

TO BE SHARED

The worst thing about being a woman is that there are always men hanging around that you don't want, waiting in the wings. In this case, I have Creep. Naturally, that was not his name, but I can't think of him as anything else. He used to work with me at the agency, but I knew there was something off about him immediately. William agreed and would often swirl around my feet in the office to steer me in the opposite direction of the rooms he was in.

Creep caught on and would find other ways to talk to me, like getting my phone number from the company directory, or chatting in my comments and DMs online. I blocked him, reported the behavior, and he was fired. Apparently, I wasn't the only one. He had shown stalking behavior to other women in the office. He will be perfect as our victim.

Still naked, I reach for my phone contacts and unblock his number. I type my address with a simple message "Bring a condom" and wait. Within moments he replies that he is on the way.

I pad to the living room and take a glass of water. William is behind me, soft touches edging me on. I whimper when his cold caress sweeps across my arm and waist. I need him and I need him now.

To distract myself, I begin to light candles around the room, referencing the color theory book I bought from The Crystal Witch, as well as the pack of colored candles for spells. I use a green candle for luck, orange for success and stamina, and purple for transformation, placing them around my bedroom. The task is done too quickly.

Twenty minutes have passed and I'm breathless on my couch, my hand pressed against my clit and aching. Nothing is good enough. I am panting and unsatisfied, in a state of hot and cold that feels like torture. My ghost feeds from me slowly, draining energy from me drip by drip to keep me ready and his channels open while we wait.

You're perfect, Emily. Such a good girl, my Emily.

I know I'll feel release soon, but my patience is thin as I am edged on until our sacrifice arrives. I am irritated, tired, and I can tell now why he can't complete this with only me. I'm already drained from this needy want and anything else would take too much from me. I'm drowning in eagerness, frustration, and waiting.

A knock sounds and I jolt. I open the door, standing behind it so my prey can't see me until he has entered the apartment. He walks through, greasy-haired and alight with what I promised him.

"Emily," he starts and then stutters at the sight of my naked, sweaty, and heaving body.

"Fuck me now," I tell the man that objectified me for weeks. Little does he know that this is not me giving in, nor is this a secret crush that I'm suddenly revealing. This is revenge. This is me taking over the situation to get what I want.

Why him? I hear William ask me, but I don't answer. He told me to bring someone desperate and that's what I did. I am giving my ghost sex-demon a large meal with this sorry excuse for a man.

In some ways, Creep gets what he wants too, but that is not a focus for me. I am here to give my lover strength and life and this asshole from my past will be a tool for me in this situation. He just doesn't know it. With assurances from William that Creep will not die, I feel no worry in taking what we need from him.

I pull him to my bedroom and position his body at the edge of the bed. He watches me, eagerly sweeping his eyes over my naked body. He opens his mouth and I hold up a finger to shush him.

"Don't speak," I demand. He closes his mouth and smiles. I hate that he seems happy that I'm taking charge, but this needs to be done. I fall to my knees in front of him and pull down his pants and underwear, seeing a small flaccid penis. I stroke him, awakening my ghost as he feeds on this man's obsession with me.

He wants you, but he could never have you. He could never handle you.

The creep opens his mouth to talk again and I roll my eyes with a huff.

"Do you want to have sex with me?" I ask him bluntly.

"Yes," he croaks. I pull my hands away from his favorite thing in the world, take off his shoes, and pull his pants down the rest of the way. I ignore his shirt. His clothes have a layer of grime, imperceptible when looking at it, but a tacky feel that points to it being more than overdue for a wash.

"Then don't talk again, not unless you change your mind. If you change your mind, tell me, and you can go." I give him the out that my morality requires. He may be consenting to have sex with me, but he does not know the rest. If he feels the drain like I do and wants to leave, then we'll let him and I'll call over my neighbor. Or order a pizza like in those weird fantasies about pizza guys getting off at a delivery. It would be weird, but there other options.

"I won't change my mind," he says with a high pitched voice echoing incredulity. I doubt it as well.

He could never resist you, William tells me. *He thinks such impure thoughts about you. Dirty, malicious things. Be safe, my angel.*

I want to reply that I know what I'm doing, but I can't with Creep listening.

This is nothing like the situation with Rosie, where she watched as I ritualistically masturbated and asked to speak with my ghost. I trusted Rosie, she felt safe and loving. I do not trust Creep to keep me safe, but I do trust him to give me what William and I need. As long as I stay in control here, and as long as he consents to the sex itself, we can accomplish our goal with him.

I push Creep to lay flat on the bed, leaving his shirt and socks on, and position my body over his now-hard dick, sheathed in the condom he had in his wallet. I remind myself to pull out, not trusting this man to have replaced his condom stash recently. Wallet condoms were not a vote of confidence.

I'm here, Emily. We'll be together soon.

Thrumming at the sound of him in my ear, I swirl my mound around the mediocre man and hum my own tune. I use his body to bring my own pleasure, chasing the feelings I want to give to my ghost. Creep feels small and skinny beneath me, which isn't turning me on. I've dated a few lanky guys, but I've always preferred bigger thighs and hard abs to grind into. My eyes are closed because I don't like the dark look of possession on his face.

Let me help, William whispers to me. A phantom hand trails along my neck and I nuzzle into it. He grows stronger and I grind into Creep. Creep groans and grabs my hips.

"You can't touch me," I growl to the body beneath me. "It's this or nothing."

"This," he chooses and pumps up his hips, driving himself faster into me, but agreeing to release his hands. He puts his hand behind his head as if he is the one getting what he wants here, satisfied by our bargain. He has no idea.

Don't let him come in you. You are mine to seed. Mine to love. Mine to hold.

"Yours," I cry.

"Yes," he hisses as if I meant him.

I notice that while his face is wide with satisfaction, he seems paler than before and his jumping hips are less enthusiastic. Is the feeding already working?

I bend down and pound my fist on the bedspread beside his head. My humble breasts graze his chin and he reaches for them with his mouth before I slap him away.

"Do I need to make you be quiet?" I hiss at the cretan.

"Yes," he asserts. "Make me."

I smile wickedly and pull back, looking forward to degrading him.

I claim you, Emily. I claim you mine, my true lover says to me.

I reach behind me and pull off one of Creep's socks. It stinks just as badly as I expected. I stuff the offending fabric into his mouth. It ignites a fire in him that I do not like, but at least he is silent.

Creep's body starts to change rhythm as I circle on top of him, pressing down and swooping to get my g-spot and rub my clit against his pelvis.

Only I will touch you from now on. My pet, my baby, my Emily.

A whisper of cold grazes my breast and I gasp, feeling him as if his body is whole. It's working, it's working!

Hold where I hold. Hide my love for you, Emily.

I reach for my breast and feel a hard invisible hand. I groan loudly, guttural in the pleasure of knowing he grows stronger and will soon be mine. His invisible hands guide mine; where he indents my skin, my fingers follow, and I feel like I'm in an intimate dance.

I land forward as William's cold caresses my back, away from the eyes of Creep. My tits fall into Creep's face and he nuzzles me, sock still in his mouth. I grab Creep's hands to stop him from reaching for my hips. I let my ghost grab them instead, pulling me up and down another man's cock while our victim's hands are above his head.

Creep makes a satisfied expression as he looks to his restrained arms. He is sweating, energy-draining from him, but yet still flushed and moaning with desire.

Creep spits the sock out of his mouth. "I'm going to come. You are so hot."

Don't let him. You are mine. He can't come inside you if you are mine, condom or not. Don't give him that pleasure.

I jump my hips up and release Creep's cock. Creep complains but I make a point to rub my backside against his length and he seems to forget that he's upset as his body spews come into the condom. I slow as he finishes, but can't help the shiver in my body.

My angel, yes, you are my good girl. Make him leave. You are mine now. Give yourself to me.

I release Creep's arms, moaning as my ghost caresses my hair and sensitive nipples, invisible and floating near but as hard as a rock. It's time for him to claim me and, boy, do I want to be claimed.

"Get out," I say to Creep. I crawl down the comforter to my pillow and lay splayed on the bedspread, vibrating with pleasure as William's touches drive me wild. A cold hard invisible finger touches my clit and I almost come at the simple touch.

"But baby, you look like you need more," Creep croons to me.

I feel my ghost behind me. He supports me, is ready for me. I stare into Creep's eyes with as much hatred as I can muster. "Get. Out." It's not until the words leave my lips that I realize my voice has taken on an echo—William is speaking through me.

Creep stumbles, getting on his pants and walks out of the room. His gait is slow, as if drunk, and I look away. Now that we have stopped touching, he is probably feeling the power and energy that was taken from him. I hear a distant, "Call me whenever" as the door closes behind him.

Mine. Angel, your life is mine, William growls in my mind.

I purr in delight, ready for whatever magic will happen next.

CHAPTER 9
ONLY MINE

"William," I moan. "Touch me. I can't wait anymore. Did it work? Do you need more? Are you full?" I ask him, praying it's enough to finish what we started.

I will never stop touching you. I won't be full until I've had you.

A shimmer presents itself to me, and I know it's him. I smile deeply, happiness exploding in me. My cunt responds in kind, waiting for him. The hovering shimmer lowers to my bed and lays its weight on me. His body is cold to the touch, but not as cold as the breeze he commands. I see a full outline, a glittering blue presence in a god-like shape. There is some detail, like the outlines of his abs and lines around his eyes, a subtle line for his lip and nose, but not the full picture.

And yet, it helps me know him. He is beautiful—utterly ridiculously beautiful. And all mine.

My Emily.

His phantom hand palms my breast again, the other reaching behind to cup my ass and angle me up. I grind my center on a delicious hardness and feel a large cock between me. I moan, unable to stop myself. I grow impossibly wetter just with the feel of his long and wide girth. It is noticeably bigger than any other penis I've handled, and I can't wait to know more about my mysterious entity and the body now available to me. Is this his full form or will this finale of our first coupling give me even more of him?

Without preamble—none are needed after our exhibitionist energy ceremony—he pushes his cock into me.

I sob at the first contact, feeling a wave of pleasure and pain. His cock is not the same as a human's. Where human flesh feels smooth, my incubus ghost's cock is rigid and thick. He's textured, tantalizing, and punishing in me, layers of ridges that get deeper and thicker the farther down I am pushed on him. I wiggle side to side, getting used to how he fills me, and yelp in surprise.

He pulls me to him and then turns our bodies over so that I am on top of his barely-visible force. His body floats up with his unknown power and we are having sex mid-air. I grip my arms around his body tightly while pulling my hips back and forth, addicted to the feel of his otherworldly cock.

"Oh, yeah. Yes, please, William. Please," I cry as I ride him. I don't know why I'm pleading, I trust him to give me more and more, but I can't stop myself.

He holds me, pushing me up as I grind down. I feel the wind that I'm used to surrounding his body. I yelp as we are pushed up into the air by the cold wind. His arms hold my ass, keeping our bodies conjoined.

I love you. I love you, his voice hums in my mind with a new quality, a gravity that is different from the last conversations we had today.

We are pure miracles. Indescribable, impossible, yet here. His body is diamond-hard beneath my hands and I feel him, luxuriating in knowing my ghost so intimately.

I grip his back and groan into his neck, arousal mixed with fear as I feel my body try to fall while we turn in the space above my bed. I quiver as we hold each other and rotate back around.

When we stabilize with me back on top, I fuck his body with all I can handle. My hands brace on his broad chest as I fall up and down his cock, crying out. I've had many orgasms this week, feeding my lover, but this feels like the biggest and most welcome one yet as my body shivers and holds his dick.

"Yes, yes, yes," I cry.

There is no awkward eye contact, no holding back

or playing it up. There is freedom in screwing an invisible man and being wholly yourself. The only downside is not knowing how he feels through his facial movement. His shivering and shimmering body sparkles around me. I reach down to stroke his face, feeling the ridge of his brow and pillowy lips.

"Are you as happy as I am right now?" I ask.

I feel words that I cannot describe. Words that I do not know. It is heaven, being with you. I have never been so happy.

He reaches for my neck and I fall into him with a hum. We share our first kiss while he is inside me. His lips kiss me delicately, adding a nibble or two that makes me gasp. He seems to like the sounds I make and slips his tongue into my mouth as he pushes harder into my hilt.

Color flies across my vision and I nearly black out as another orgasm overtakes me. How many has it been now? I clench around his thick rigid cock, knowing I'm ruined for any other mortal man.

My Emily, he repeats, nuzzling into my neck. I pant against him, rocking slowly back and forth as my body calms down. We slowly float back onto the bed, no longer suspended by his unearthly power. When we land, he flips me again so he is on top.

Do you want to be with me forever, Emily?

"Yes," I whisper. His soft lips lap on mine.

He pushes my legs up over my head and over his

shoulders. I feel a delicious stretch as he pushes deeper into me.

His long limb sheathes in me over and over, an even pace of shuddering fullness as each ridge pushes into me. I lift myself into his thrusts, my arms running up and down his back, feeling his head and finding what feels like hair. I sigh into him, pulling his face toward mine.

I hold my hands on his face, touching his eyebrows, the ridge of his nose, trailing his neck. He feels real to me because somehow he is real. This dream is my reality now. But as I look, all I see is a shimmer in the air and the bedroom around me. He kisses me and I can't help but to sigh into his mouth. We kiss for several long minutes, dancing our tongues together while he holds himself still in me.

I feel a groan trapped in his throat, a real expression of him that isn't in my head. I keep my hand hovering above his Adam's apple. This isn't the end, there is more, more, more strength for him to gain now that he is in this act with me.

It's even better than I imagined it would be, his voice whispers to me.

"It feels good to me too," I say into his lips, his ice cold body bringing me to another orgasm. "I-I-lov—"

My words are cut off by his tongue and I shiver as I ride the high of my pulsating body.

There is a way we can be together, in your world.

Where I can have a true face for you to look upon, his mind tells me while our lips still touch.

"How?" I pull back to ask, daring to hope that we can have more. I will do anything to have this connection, this intimacy, every day.

By anchoring me to the earth, by having my baby.

CHAPTER 10
BABY, BABY

"I-I—" I stutter again for entirely different reasons than my lust-filled confusion before. I have always wanted to be a mother. When these feelings started developing for William, part of me realized if that continued I would never be one. Now he was saying it's a possibility. Can I truly have all that I want in the end? Can I bring a child into a loving, but supernatural, home?

"But how can we have a baby? How is that even possible?" I am, after all, currently being fucked by an incubus ghost. I assume his considerably different member has to do with his demon status, rather than his ghost one, but I'm not following how this could even happen.

It is you and me. We are not possible, yet we are here.

Our baby will be you and me. Perfect. Magic finds a way, just like it did when it brought us together.

I moan again, unable to stop the pleasure coursing through me as he calls us perfect. I force myself to ask questions, trying to stay focused with my legs hiked up and delicious pressure filling me one notch of ridges at a time.

"Will the baby be okay being only half human?" I hold my breath, worried that this dream will shatter.

Yes, our love protects them. The baby will be special, but they will be whole.

I shiver as a chill flows through my body, up from my toes to my brow. It feels peaceful and sensual, like goosebumps from a breeze or a caress. I reason with myself and the pounding of my heart. Nothing about this situation is normal. No psychic is going to help me with this answer. For all I know, this is the only time this has ever happened in the universe, or it could be more common than I know. Without a doubt, this is the decision Rosie told me to watch out for. This is my crossroads.

"How do you know it will anchor you?" I ask. If it didn't and I had his child alone, I would still be happy, but it would not be the same. I need to know the whole picture.

For my kind, it's not just sexual energy, but creation. Making a child is the most potent energy there is. It's a connection that can never be severed. It will work.

I focus inward. This life altering decision...how does it feel? It feels scary and right. Scary, and yet safe at the same time. He's mine. William and the baby. I know that even if I have to think about it for weeks, I will still say yes. It's insane to consider this now, but I won't turn it down.

Will you let me love you forever, Emily? Will you let us have a baby? Can I come for the first time in your beautiful body? Can we raise a family together?

He pushes harder into my hilt with each question and I cry out, reaching up and gripping his invisible back with my finger nails. Our bodies pulse together and I so desperately want it all. I stare into the shimmering outline above me and run my fingers along his jaw and smile.

"Yes, yes, let's have a baby. Stay with me."

I give in, but it isn't hard to. My logical brain tells me that this shouldn't be, that it makes no sense, and if it works, something could go really wrong. I shut that part away. This isn't just lust speaking to me, this is divine intervention. We are a certain magic that has always been meant to be. I take the leap, the uncontrollable urge now released.

I am meant to bring this being and its child into the world. They chose me and I chose them.

His body shivers and I know he is about to let go. He comes into me, filling me like I am meant to be filled. Energy soars between us and I know instantly that something is different. He seems more solid, the edges in front of me more opaque.

"Don't stop, it's working," I cry. "Give all of it to me."

You and me. You and me. You and me, he repeats as he fills me up. I feel strength coursing through me. Love. Safety. I'm stronger, full of life in a way I've never experienced before. This marathon moment—that is what it feels like with the hours of pleasure that have passed since this morning—will be imprinted on my mind forever. Nothing this good could be bad.

You and me, his spirit continues to sing to me like a beating drum. I meet his rhythm, pulling in whatever is equivalent to spiritual semen with my thrusts, quivering. I'm coming again, possessed by him and his need to fill me. He gently folds my legs back down, caressing me as I calm down.

"Mine, mine, mine," I whisper to my ghost, my spirit, my William, and let myself be filled with his magic.

His spirit takes form, his body now outlined in white, pulling from the energy of our love. His body pulses, pushing into me endlessly as we both groan together. My hands trace his stomach and up his broad shoulders. More details come into view, more than what I could feel and see just moments ago. His delicious neck pulses with visible veins and shaggy bangs fall over his deep eyes.

I see more and more of him and I keen, purring as I push my hips up so my clit hits his pelvic bone.

Rather than hearing his inner voice, his throat begins to work in the 3D realm as he solidifies and a true moan erupts from his body.

"My Emily," he says in our world, his first true words, and pulls me in for a gentle kiss. "I'm here. I'll always be here."

CHAPTER II
FOREVER

When our emotions and bodies finally calm, all that is left is to stare. Tangled together on my sweaty sheets, I have William. He is real and mine forever. My favorite music would now always be his heartbeat in my ear.

"Are you sure this is real?" I can't help but ask. It's a culmination of years of peace and a heightened period of arousal, but now William is a reality not unlike all the other pieces of my world. He has always been with me and now, nothing can keep us apart.

"It's surreal, but yes. I'm here, my Emily."

I sit up so I can get a better look at him. I'm in awe, finally seeing and speaking with the presence I've known all my life.

William has brown shaggy straight hair that falls into his face and brown deep eyes. He's a bit pale, but does vitamin D matter to a ghost? I really want to touch his muscles again, but I'm also confused about how they got there. And his dick, my god...this is a beast. My eyes trail down his torso to his cock. Even partially soft, it is thick and shaped in layers that grow thicker as it reaches the base. I never thought I would want a dick full of layers of ridges, but here we are and I'm not turning back. He puts "ribbed for her pleasure" condoms to shame.

"You are gorgeous," I blurt out.

William laughs and pulls me back down to his chest. "Glad you think so," he says and I hear the pleasant rumble of his voice against me.

"Were you working out as a ghost?" I ask, unable to ignore that curiosity.

"No, I wasn't a normal ghost as you have gathered. Because our energy was tied together and I grew up with you, my mind and body changed also. I think it's just driven by my mind. I don't know if this is how I would have looked if I were alive this whole time or if I made it up. But I have muscles, so I guess I'll have to start going to the gym now to keep it." He seems amazed, wondrous, and unwilling to let me go. I look up from my position leaning on his chest and find him staring down at me with a gentle smile and a twinkle in his eye.

I giggle into his chest, smiling and thinking how silly that predicament is. "I'd love to just become muscular because I thought so." I think again and ask, "Were you naked the whole time you were a ghost?"

"No, I don't make the ghost rules or anything, and I know I was both alive and dead, which is confusing... but I would imagine myself in different outfits and I'd suddenly be wearing them. Same with the muscles." He pulls me closer and kisses my hair. "Magic is typically the answer to every question I don't know."

"Did you manifest your dick to be this fucking magical?" I snort and reach my hand down, trailing up his length. He immediately grows hard again and shivers against me. It's nice to know I have the same effect on him as he does on me.

"Hm, no, that is what it's supposed to look like for an incubus," he explains, voice breathy with distraction. "For succubi women, their cunts are more of a vice grip than usual. We are all wired to make sex more pleasurable as an evolutionary imperative."

"If feeding on sexual energy is such an imperative, do you need to feed on a lot of other people by having sex with them? Or watching them have sex?" I needed to know what was a requirement versus a preference.

He chuckles, deep and throaty, nuzzling back into my neck. His piece between us rubs against my ass. I subconsciously lean into it and he purrs against my neck.

"No. My Emily, you are enough for me. I don't need to be fed sex to stay alive, but I am the most myself when I have been satiated. Being a succubus doesn't mean you are promiscuous, it's just an option. Some succubi and incubi are in open relationships, but many aren't. Many people get into sex work too because it's an accessible avenue to have that around you. Like running a sex club, or working at a strip club, even using fan websites to draw in people watching you and taking their energy through live chats. Technically, it doesn't even have to be sex, it's about passion and creation. Sex, art, really caring about what you are doing and feeling passion in it, pregnancy, all of it would feed me."

"So earlier with Creep doesn't need to be a regular thing?" The note about art was certainly interesting. I've never seen that when people add succubi to plots on TV.

"No, we don't need to have three-ways or any other experiences, not unless you want to experiment. I'd do any of that for you and with you. I need a lot of power and energy to accomplish coming back and taking from two people made the feeding easier on both of your bodies. Though, I admit, I took the most from him. He likely felt like he had the worst hangover of his life afterward. I'm not versed in incubus demon ghost resurrections, so we're guessing a lot here. I've based a lot on just what I heard from my parents. I only recently started feeding; my feeding drive was delayed for me as a ghost."

"Speaking of incubus demon ghosts resurrections and kids," I say the tongue-twister slowly. "For humans, we don't just immediately get pregnant the second come enters our pussy. How would what we just did make you alive again when the sperm could not have possibly attached to my egg yet? Is it different for sex demons?"

His hands trail up my naked back and he hums, looking me in the eye. "I hate saying I don't know the answer again or just blaming it on magic, but what I do know is that pregnancy is the ultimate creation energy and is the most potent for my kind. We get pregnant in the same way. But I thought, if that energy was tied between us, it would keep me here. And it seemed to work because we intended it too. Are you happy it did?"

His arm snakes across my back, pulling me closer to him and up his body. He nuzzles my neck and I sigh, leaning into him. There is still so much to talk about and sort through, especially now that he is human. Or, as human as he can be.

"I'm so happy it worked. I'm so happy you are here. I could stare at you for years. I would touch you for decades, unendingly, if it meant you would stay here with me."

He holds me gently, running his hands over my back as he tells me more about his powers and what it will mean for our child should they inherit them. I feel worried that being a succubus would mean they would grow up too fast, getting children involved in a sexual world they should not be in.

Thankfully that's not the case. Their need to feed will not start for them until their twenties. When they are younger they may feel possessiveness with their friends and their family, but there will be time to help them cope with that and what they may deal with in the future.

I have so much to learn about what a sex demon, and our family, will need. I've never been more excited to learn.

CHAPTER 12
KINSHIP

The day has passed quickly. We solved a few problems quickly, like ordering him clothing and a toothbrush for same-day delivery, but there is a lot that will take days and even weeks to solve.

Our conversation shifts back to his years as a ghost as I cook up a storm. While sex gives him the most energy, William still needs food in his body to survive, and it's been years since he has eaten as a human. I've been running around the kitchen making pretty much every frozen food in my freezer and some scrambled eggs. I hope it's good enough since I'm not much of a cook.

"What did you do each day," I ask.

"Usually I'm watching you wherever you are. Sometimes, I'd check up on people you know. If I thought of someone, I would somehow be where they were," he says as he tries a bite of mac and cheese.

"Really, that's a cool power. Like who?" I'd be so nosey if I could do that and would visit everyone I met in high school. Or celebrities. I'd take advantage of that at all hours.

His answer comes hesitantly. "Your mom and dad mostly. I can think of them and suddenly be where they are. Or, I could before. I guess that is gone now." My dad...I haven't seen him for over a decade, not since the divorce. I don't even have his new number, yet it's likely William has seen him multiple times since then.

"How is Mom doing?" I ask, seeing that as the easiest question.

"Good, same as when you last talked to her. Mostly plays bingo, works, and goes home."

I nod. That's expected. And I don't even need the answer, I gathered that already from her Facebook page. I take the last microwave dinner out of the microwave and arrange it on the kitchen island with the eggs and other plates. He has six meals to eat between him and he tries a little of each as we talk.

"And how is my dad?" I ask nervously, holding my breath. I try not to think of him most days, but when you've been abandoned, that wound tends to fester the more it is ignored.

William pauses before answering. He knows what

life was like with my dad. "He is both the same and different from how you remember him. You still wouldn't like him."

"Why do you think that?" If William knows me so well, he is likely right. But this statement makes me worry. I move around the island to sit beside him and pick up my own fork. He is wearing my baggy pants that I take out when I'm sick. They look like regular sweatpants on him and sexy as hell with his bare chest.

"He is remarried and has another daughter. She is only a little younger than you," William admits, turning to watch my face.

"Oh…" My emotions spiral into a traitorous rage. I wanted him to be unhappy, unloved, and alone. Yet, having another daughter? Does he treat her better? Is it just me he doesn't want? How much younger? Did he cheat on my mom?

"Her name is Kiera. She also doesn't like him," William tells me.

"So, I have a sister." I've always wanted one but hadn't expected it would happen like this.

"Yes. I can tell you about her if you want," he offers, tracing a hand up my shoulder and pulling me into a side hug. I lean back into him, scooting my chair closer.

"No, no." I shake my head. "I'd rather get to know

her in person, but thank you for telling me. I wouldn't have ever known I had a sister if you hadn't."

My voice cracks with emotion. There is so much I hate my father for, but this jumps to the top of the list. To keep family from me, to ditch us only to make a new unit we aren't involved in...I will never forgive him.

I turn my attention back to William. As much as I want to dissect this new information and wonder what makes me less worthy of my father's time than his new family, I stop myself. I can learn more about Kiera another day. Now, I am given the chance to get to know my oldest friend. I am not going to waste it.

"What were your parent's like?" I want to hit myself for not asking until now. He isn't the only one who was taken from this world. His parents were killed in front of him, and then he was alone.

"More perfect than I realized, until they weren't there with me. I've had so much time to think about them and realize all the small things they did for me and each other. So much that I didn't see when we were all alive and well. I miss them," William says. He abandons his fork on the table and pulls me in closer again.

We move to the couch and talk for hours about them and what it was like to be a child in a succubi household. He describes his parents as always hugging and kissing each other's cheek, going out several times a week on dates that he suspects were actually sex parties.

"That must have been awkward. I'd hate knowing about my parent's sex life," I comment.

"It was, because who wants to know that? But it was also a normal part of our culture. I was always sheltered from it, but they spent time explaining things to me so that I would be prepared. It isn't just sex, like I told you, it's creation and life energy. Especially in my younger years, they encouraged me to try different sports, art projects, to make friendships. Some friendships were harder than others because you have a tendency to get jealous when born into this type of energy demon family."

"You've mentioned that a lot, little comments here and there about energy that seems bigger than what you've told me." I'm curious. I wish there were some guides I could reference.

"All supernatural creatures deal with energy in some way. Whether it be like me with creation, passion, and sex, or vampires that crave the life energy that comes from blood. There are demons that crave the energy of destruction and death, or energy pulled from the sun in plants. Others simply move energy around rather than keeping it, like a muse. It's everywhere. I say energy, but it is intent, subatomic particles. Magic. There are so many ways to describe it. In the end, we are all particles of something on this rock in space and we explain it all differently, like religion."

"It sounds so beautiful. We are all connected," I say. I don't follow any one religion, but I see how they all have similarities. From what William has told me, it's the same for all beings.

"We are. We are all energy," he says with a gesture between our bodies. "And with that, we can all be transmuted, transformed, transferred, all of that. Almost everything in life is an energy exchange, but for people like me, it's in a more literal sense."

"Because energy isn't created or destroyed," I muse, knowing that is a science quote I've heard before but can't place. I'll have to Google it later.

"Yes, exactly, my parents taught me that. That life is a balance. For our species, our balance is in the act of love. They are really protective too. Most paranormals know that there is the possibility of being hunted. We have a secret bank account and home that I now have access to. We'll have to go find our broker soon."

"You just came to life and now you tell me you have a house and money put aside? That's handy," I muse, impressed by the amount of planning that needs. Paranoia, too. Is our baby in danger just for existing and will need something similar prepared?

"A lot about being paranormal isn't convenient, so

we try and make up for it where we can. I'm grateful for it now, we'll have more resources for our family, but I wish it wasn't needed. I wish my parents were here." William's voice catches and I grip his hand tighter.

"I'm so sorry you lost them. I wish I could have met them," I say, wishing that they too had been ghosts in the afterlife with him.

"They would have liked you," he whispers, brushing a strand of hair behind my ear.

With the little he described of his parents so far, I love seeing these qualities already in him. He is attentive, like he described his parents as, I wonder if he notices that about himself yet.

We hold each other for some time, forgetting food and the other things we said we'd work on today. A knock on the door sounds and I go to it, picking up the bag of clothes from our delivery. William helps me clear out a drawer in my room and we place in his things. It's not much, but enough for a few days.

I can't believe I just brought back a ghost from the dead, he is moving in with me, and I'm having his baby.

"Are succubi pregnancies different in any way? Is there anything I need to know?" I ask, looking down at the bloat from my food and lack of hydration, rather than a baby bump. *Note to self, drink a lot more water.*

"You'll crave sex more than certain foods," he says. "The sexual energy between us is tied to creation and fertility. It will help the baby grow strong."

"That doesn't sound too bad," I comment, smiling up at him.

"No, I don't think so either," he says and pulls me back to him, his eyes grazing down my cleavage.

"You really are a boob guy," I say, but not minding the attention.

"These are the only breasts I've touched, but I think you are right," he admits.

"I was so wrapped up in all that has happened, being with you as a ghost, having that odd three-way, then deciding to get pregnant right away, that I forgot that you died before experiencing these things. I'm sorry, I should have talked to you more about that. Are you okay? Was it what you expected?" I tap my fingers on his chest and worry my lip, realizing I should have paid more attention to this earlier.

"Even better than I expected, my angel. Every moment with you is the heaven I was denied."

We hug each other in the middle of my small bedroom, chest to chest. He sighs into my hair and says, "I look forward to dreaming tonight. I haven't slept in years."

"I wonder what your first dream will be like. Being awake twenty-four seven sounds exhausting."

"After a while my brain would shut off, like when you are staring off into space and go a bit numb. But often I just had my thoughts for hours while you slept," William explains.

"Let's take a nap now," I muse and tug him to the bed. He hums into my hair and we cuddle, my arm snaking around his bare chest. His body still runs cold to the touch, so we pile the blankets back on top of us to keep me warm. But truthfully, I don't mind. If he makes me shiver all my life, I will be so lucky.

"What is your favorite color?" I ask him after listening happily to his heart for a few beats. His deep laugh shakes my head and I smile widely.

"It feels like we are both past that and not. I know your favorite color is purple. I know so much about you, and while my lens of the world has been through yours, there are some things that we think differently on that I can't wait to tell you. My favorite color is green."

"I'm glad to finally get to hear your side, William." I look forward to nothing else.

"Will you marry me, Emily?"

Tears spring to my eyes and there is no hesitation as I say, "Of course, I will."

We fall asleep, and when we wake up, William tells me he dreamt of me. We talk for a while before I spend some time exploring William's incubus cock with my mouth, finding I can only fit up to the fourth ridge comfortably. Getting the final one to fit makes my mouth too wide and it is difficult to breathe, so I save it for the big finale. He shows me how much he appreciates the effort as I bob through each layer, his eyes rolling back into his head.

What a world, what a life, what a love.

CHAPTER 13
TREASURED

William and I have decided on a long engagement. We have already spent years together, but being together physically and able to communicate with our voices and bodies is new. We aren't in a rush to make it official, especially when William is listed legally as deceased. He says his family broker can help with that, but it will take a few weeks. Thankfully, he'll be a legal person before our baby is born so I can list him on the birth certificate.

I look down at my pear-shaped engagement ring and smile. I did end up taking Monday off of work and we went to a jewelry store at William's insistence. We started to sort out his inheritance too, getting all that we needed together for our new life. His broker was certainly surprised to see him again, alive and all grown up. He had kept his word to the family and the money and home were still available to William. We didn't go into many details, and he didn't seem to need them. The broker explained that in his line of work, families occasionally go into hiding or fake their deaths, and it was better that he didn't know why. Neither is the case for William, but I didn't correct him.

Unfortunately, I couldn't take off today as well. George has been preparing for this client meeting and needs my help. I want to take it seriously, but I can't stop grinning. I don't know how much help I'll be today with all this giddiness.

The office is certainly in for a surprise. We aren't sharing the pregnancy yet, partially because I won't one hundred percent believe I'm magically pregnant until I miss my period, but I also want to enjoy it in privacy for a few weeks. I'm not one to believe sharing your pregnancy early is bad luck—that's such a personal decision for each couple to make—but I will not be quiet about my engagement.

Not that many people will *actually* care. I don't have friends here, just people that are cordial, but at least I can enjoy being part of some nice gossip. I won't deny it's nice to be talked about. And when they see my man? They'll be jealous. I don't connect with people often, and I've gotten used to that, but knowing I have my ghost with me forever feels worth the loneliness of all the years before. This isn't something anyone else will ever have or experience, and I feel so lucky.

I park and look at William, who insisted on coming with me to work. He can't drive, so we made a list of things he can do in the area to get ready for life as a human. Well, he was never human, but to prepare his life as a living being again after so many years. He needed more clothes, a wallet, shoes, so much. It was pretty hilarious when we calmed down from our coupling to find there was nothing for him to wear. My office area is a hub of stores, so he should be able to find a lot of what he needs. I can't wait to meet him for lunch.

He walks me to my building hand in hand. I keep looking up at his brown eyes and smiling, in disbelief that this is my life now. I get to be loved, as I am, and I get to love someone wholly back. We stand to the side of the door and he wraps me in his arms. This will technically be the first time we've been apart. While he has visited other members of my family as a ghost, it was for short moments. He has spent the majority of his life with me and now we have to live as people, without his shivering wind beside me all the time. It's surreal and sad. That part of our life is over. I'm grateful, but I will miss his constant protection and companionship.

"I can't believe you have to go in that building and

be away from me all day," he groans, reaching down to nuzzle and kiss my neck. I sigh into his embrace, wanting nothing more than to turn around and go back to our apartment.

"I know. I'm going to miss you," I whine and pout my lips. He lifts his head and pulls my bottom lip into his mouth with his teeth. Our lips entertain us for several long minutes and I momentarily forget that I'm supposed to be working until I hear a pointed cough behind us.

I reluctantly let go and glance behind me to see George staring at us with an eyebrow raised. He looks more amused than disapproving. He's dressed in a suit today for the presentation, his deep green tie complementing his reddish-brown skin.

"You coming in today, Emily?"

"Yes." I grin sheepishly. "George, meet my fiancé, William."

"Oh!" George says in surprise. "Nice to meet you, William." As they shake hands, William keeps his other on my back.

"I'll see you at lunch, angel," William tells me and dips down for another peck. He calmly walks down the street as if it's something he's done thousands of times and I sigh staring after him.

"You look very smitten right now," George comments and opens the door for me.

"Yes, I am," I admit, unable to keep the blush from my neck.

"I didn't know you were seeing someone," he says when we get in the elevator.

I tell him the story of partial truths William and I came up with. "I've known him all my life, we met in elementary school and kept in touch throughout the years. Then when we finally decided to go for it, it was like we were meant to be and things progressed pretty quickly."

I can't keep the smile off my face. I bounce on my heels as the elevator climbs to our floor. George congratulates me and we exit to our desks. I begin to count down the hours to lunch, already desperate to be in William's arms again.

I FLY OUT OF THE OFFICE AND FIND WILLIAM ALREADY waiting outside. I jump into his arms and wrap my legs around his torso. He grips me back with a laugh and says, "Happy to see you too."

I smile brightly at him. "It was more exhausting than usual to be at work. I'm so used to feeling you with me, I found myself so hot because I'm used to your cold."

He laughs with me and I hop down. We hold hands and walk down to my favorite cafe. I spot a few coworkers sneaking glances and I don't blame them. I'm so private and guarded at work, this is juicy news, and honestly, my man is so beautiful.

As we wait in line for my usual panini and chai tea, I tell him the options he has to choose from. For every few, he leans in to whisper something in my ear or smell my hair. Every small moment of normalcy centers me in a universe where love conquers all and I treasure it more than words can say.

He eats his food quickly and tries some of mine. After so long in the afterlife, there is a lot to re-experience, and I welcome every moment that I get to do it with him.

"Let me show you some of the things I got while you were working," he says after we finish up. He opens the door for me and puts his arm around my shoulders. I lean into his side, walking to the car to see what he stashed there. Before we get there, he pulls me down the alley instead.

"Wha—" I'm silenced by his lips. I moan into them, kissing back greedily. His hands pull my legs up and around him, my back leaning against the building. His weight settles against me, showing he has been just as eager as I have felt all day.

His hardness rubs against my center and my panties dampen. I feel so ever grateful that I wore my flowy skirt that ends at my knees rather than the pencil skirt or my pants. I'll have to rethink my clothing for these encounters.

I keen, trapped against him and excited about the possibility of being caught. He leads us farther down the alley, but if anyone glanced over while walking by, they will know.

"Are you going to be quiet for me, angel?" William asks as he reaches one hand to undo his zipper.

"Yes," I whisper, exhilarated and worried at the same time.

He pushes my underwear to the side and positions his cock at my entrance.

"Do you want me to fuck you in this alley?" he questions me, each tantalizing word a whisper in my ear.

I nod *yes*, unable to form words, and he pushes one notch in. I bite my lip and whimper. He pushes another notch of his ribbed dick forward and I gasp. In this position, I can feel him hitting new deep spots that I have never experienced before.

I wrap my legs tighter and pull him to me with my thighs, forcing him in two notches forward.

I pant, losing my breath over the way he stretches me. He pulls out his four notches, rubbing against my walls and I whine. Before I ask him why, he pushes back in to the hilt of his fifth notch and I nearly scream in pleasure. I clamp my teeth on his shoulder to keep myself quiet and the world explodes in stars.

He pulls in and out, praising me in whimpers, calling me his angel, until there is very little left of me conscious of anything but our combined joy and throbbing. When he finally slows, his own orgasm seated in me, the sounds of the city come back and I glance around to make sure we haven't been seen.

"How am I supposed to go back to work now?" I ask with a pant. He drops his forehead to mine and our noses touch. We breathe together for a moment before he answers.

"Simple, you will pull your underwear back in place and walk there as my come drips down your leg," William says.

I had meant emotionally, because being with him was supremely better than being away from him, but I take his instructions to heart.

He gently releases me and zips his cock back into his pants. I slide back down the wall and do precisely as instructed. We make a stop so he can actually show me what he purchased and I'm impressed with all he did in such a short amount of time. We still need to get his cell phone set up on my phone plan, but we'll do that together after work. For now, he plans to join the gym on the next block over and use his new workout clothes while I finish up.

As I walk back to the office, I have to stop twice to wipe my leg with one of the portable makeup wipes from my purse.

CHAPTER 14
THE DOCTOR IS IN
THREE MONTHS LATER

I did end up missing my period and getting a positive pregnancy test. I had been acting under the assumption that I was pregnant, making sure not to drink and to be more conscious of eating healthy and drinking water. I started taking prenatal vitamins, too. But since I had no symptoms in those first few weeks, it didn't feel real. The test helped solidify that for me and we started thinking about names and planning life with a baby. The symptoms have definitely ramped up since then.

I am three months pregnant now and William and I have been insatiable. There isn't a day that goes by where he isn't making me come on his incubus cock and his cold tongue. With his cock made to be extra pleasurable, that has been an asset in my pregnancy cravings. *That* is a smart evolutionary update for a sex demon, and I'm happy to benefit from it.

He has told me that this is normal for a succubus pregnancy. There are some days when he takes me four separate times, not because he wants to—though he certainly does—but more so because I'm constantly horny. I didn't realize how annoying that could be. In the moment with William, it's perfect, but waiting for William when we aren't together? Torture.

It got in the way at work. I needed to take breaks to masturbate in the bathroom or have sex with William in our car, at the gym, and even in the alley multiple times. It became too much, and at two months pregnant I decided to quit my job. I'm sure I'll work again after things have settled and the baby is born, but for now, I'm not in a rush. With William's inheritance, I have time to decide when or if I'll go back.

I've learned so much about the supernatural since William came into the 3D world. There is so much I didn't know about the world we live in. So many people do not know what is going on all around us. Now when we walk down the street, William points out to me other creatures that he can sense as an energy being.

I'm not sure about when we'll want to move into the house William's parents left him. It feels so big and out of the way. Me and my ghost enjoy our apartment for now and there is plenty of room for a crib. Maybe when the baby is walking around, we'll leave. Toddlers in an apartment are a nightmare for all involved.

I pad naked back into the bedroom with our breakfast and find William tossing in bed. I gently pat his shoulder and he startles awake, breathing heavily.

"Did you have a nightmare?" I ask him and soothe the crinkle along his brow.

"Yes," he says and pulls me on my arm. I abandon the food on a tray on the floor and cuddle into his side. He scoops me in, holding me tightly in place. It must have been a bad one this time. His nightmares have come up a few times since he came back to life. I've noticed he has at least one a week, but I think there are more that he doesn't tell me about.

"Today is going to be a great day, we're all safe, and we'll get to see our baby for the first time. Don't worry, baby," I tell him, running my hands through his hair. He nods into my bare chest, nuzzling my breasts. I feel the hunger grow in me, but I do my best to ignore it. We have an appointment to get to. "Get up and eat baby, we have to leave in twenty minutes."

I try to pull from his embrace but before I do, he gives my breasts an appreciative squeeze. I groan and arc my back, panting, but I slap his hand back and pull away again.

"Don't distract me," I scowl and get off the bed. I throw on a simple wrap dress. He smirks at me and eats what I prepared for him. There is no time to pause and I don't want to be late for our doctor. Not like last time.

Thank goodness she is a supernatural OB-GYN. She is used to a lot of weird requests, knows our unique needs, and understands some of the tendencies of families in this position. When I became pregnant, William reached out to his former pediatrician and thankfully he was still in business and knew a supernatural OB-GYN specialist, so we've been seeing her and going over different succubi milestones so I would know what to expect. Dr. Bones has been a delight.

We arrive in the office and I twist my ring nervously, hoping they say everything is as it should be with our baby.

"The doctor will be with you shortly," the nurse comments and hands me the gown to change into. The door closes and I sigh, brow furrowing.

"Allow me, angel," William says and takes the gown from my hands. He guides me into the middle of the room and kneels, taking off each sandal. His hands rub my calves more than what is necessary and I quiver.

"She'll be here any moment," I whisper and glance at the door.

"Yes, she will," he replies and looks up into my eyes, his hands inching up my dress.

I whimper, staring back as he cups my ass before reaching for the string that holds the dress together.

"I have to take care of my family," he tells me, standing to pull it off my shoulders and letting the fabric fall to the floor.

He kisses me and I sigh into him. One hand reaches for my mound, cupping me, and instinctively I push myself forward.

"We shouldn't do this," I try to protest again, but I know it's fruitless. My body has already decided it needs more.

William reaches behind me for the gown and helps me into it. After he is done, he guides me to the table I'm supposed to lay down on. Carrying me up, he sits me on the edge, and puts my legs in the stirrups.

"What are you doing?" I ask, panting.

"I told you. Taking care of my family."

His head dives beneath the gown and his cold mouth meets the most sensitive parts of me. I cover my mouth to muffle the cry that begs to escape.

He licks me from bottom to top, swirling his tongue over my clit and repeating the motion. He groans, going faster, reaching one hand up to keep that pressure while his tongue fucks me. I buck up into him, panting, keening, and nearly scream as my heel pushes harder into the cold metal.

I come on his mouth, the fastest he has ever tipped me over, and he laps up my arousal. I hear someone walking down the hall and I'm about to push him off me when his body jumps up and I see his other hand is pounding his hard rigid cock.

Wide-eyed, I watch him stroke and bite my lip in anticipation. He pushes up the gown and aims for my pussy, inserting his tip and releasing his seed in me. He feeds it to me and I quiver, enjoying the cold dripping in and out of me. He pulls out, satisfied, and uses his fingers to push in all the leaking fluid.

"Keep your hips up, angel, or you'll leak and I'll have to start again."

My eyes glaze over as I follow his instructions, aroused. He puts his magnanimous incubi cock back into his pants and sits on the chair at the right of my head, as calm he can be. A door closes across the hall and voices get closer. A knock sounds on the door as loud as my racing heart and our doctor walks in, a wide smile on her face.

"Great news, your blood test results came back. Would you like to know the sex of the baby before we get started? It's too early to know from the scan, but the test can tell us the answer."

"Of course," I say, already teary-eyed and gripping William's hand.

"You're having a girl," she says, coming farther into the room and getting her gloves on. William and I look at each other, smiling. We didn't care either way, any answer would have been such a blessing, but knowing I can give a girl the upbringing I needed makes me want to cry all over again.

We go over my symptoms, to my embarrassment also discussing how often I want sex, but after working with multiple succubi pregnancies she assures me it's normal.

"Okay, it's going to be a little pinch and the liquid will be cold, but once we get situated we'll be able to see the baby."

She covers the wand in a plastic bag and coats it with the medical-approved lube, and lifts the gown to expose my entrance. I can tell by the slight hesitation that she can tell we've just had sex, but moves on quickly and inserts the wand. I blush, knowing she is pushing into the semen pooled in me, but get distracted quickly by what's on the screen.

We look at the monitor together, at a baby that looks like barely anything this early in, and I can't help but cry a third time. William brushes the top of my head like I'm a cat, trying to soothe me. Everything looks as expected and she congratulates us again.

"I'll give you two a minute to yourselves," the doctor says, handing William the photo printout, "and then come meet the receptionist to set your follow-up appointment."

We express our gratitude and I wipe my tears as the door closes.

"We made a baby," I say meekly as William helps

me up from the table. I feel a drip of his seed roll down my thigh.

"We did, my angel, and we'll make many more."

He pulls me into my arms, his finger reaching for the leaking seed, trailing it back up and sticking his finger in to reinsert what left my body without permission.

"I love you," I say to William like a pleading prayer.

"I love you," he whispers back and removes my gown. He helps me dress again, peppering me with kisses.

We set up our next visit, leave the office, and make love on the floor of our apartment for many hours after.

CHAPTER 15

LIFE

ONE MONTH LATER

Things with my mother are slowly getting better. We've talked for a few minutes each week on the phone, and she has visited once to meet William. I think she likes him. We are far from best friends, but she is excited to be a grandmother. The only problem is she told my dad. I didn't even know she still has his active number. I would have been happy to never speak to him again. I'm supposed to meet with him while he is in town next week. I'm not looking forward to it and neither is William. He has been antsy since I told him and hovering more. In a way, my dad hurt him too. Every time my dad made me cry, William was there to comfort me. He has all those experiences with me and naturally feels angry.

"Let's go out today," I tell him when I walk into the kitchen. He has been figuring out what he likes and doesn't like food-wise, so trying new restaurants has been fun. We both need to get some vitamin D, so I think about what may be close by. Maybe we'll try that new restaurant that opened a few blocks away. The doctor has said walking is good for me. I'm sure all the sex counts as exercise, but I still need to move my body more and a short walk will be nice.

"I'd love too," he says and reaches for my hips. Quickly, I'm backed into the countertop and he cups me through my yoga pants.

"I'm serious," I say and wiggle out of his grip. He knows that once I get going, it's hard for me to turn away. These pregnancy hormones are intense.

"So am I. We'll go right after I eat you."

"Oh, my incubus needs a feeding?" I purr, gripping his chin so he can stare back into my eyes instead of at the peak of my swelling breasts.

"Mmhm," he hums, nodding up and down.

"Will you be a good boy and let me go out and play first?" I ask.

"What do I get if I behave?" he has the audacity to ask.

I reach and tug the hair at the nape of his neck and breathe into his ear, "Whatever I decide to give you."

He growls into my neck and my underwear is immediately soaked. I love when he is feral.

"Let's go so you can earn a present," I whisper, already losing resolve.

He nibbles and whines into my neck before pulling back. The second he sees my face he smiles, seeming pleased at the sight of my red neck and my pouty lips. He knows he got to me, but he's letting me take control for the moment.

We slip our shoes on, agree on the restaurant, and head out to the elevator. We have the space to ourselves so he distracts me some more. I want to curl into his cashmere sweater and stay there all day. I bite my lip and he pulls away when the *ding* of the first floor sounds.

"Who the fuck is that?" A familiar voice demands. We turn around and William blocks my body from moving with his strong arms.

"Damen, what are you doing here?" I ask, using Creep's real name for once, seeing him from behind William's safety.

"I came to see you since you stopped answering me again. I was worried, and I find you with another man?" His voice is filled with unfounded incredulity. He's delusional if he thinks he has rights to my well-being after a one-night stand months ago.

"We were not seeing each other, Damen. It was a one-night thing and you know that," I say. I'd never regret using him to bring William back—it worked after all—but I didn't expect him to try and re-enter my life afterward. William's arms shake slightly and I wonder what he is thinking about in this scenario.

"I should have known what a slut you were," Damen sneers, looking at William instead of me.

"Don't," William warns, an edge to his voice I've never heard before.

"Don't what? Been there, done that," Damen spits.

Willian bolts forward, grabbing Creep by the neck and forcing him against the elevator door. "You will never speak to her again, you hear me?" he sneers.

"I wasn't planning on talking to her anyway. I was here to see her ass in the air."

William snarls and grips Creep's neck harder. Damen coughs and gasps. William tightens his hold again and Damen grows quiet, wide-eyed with tears streaming at the loss of circulation.

"I'm going to count to five. During this count-down, you are going to imagine your life flash before your eyes. It will be pathetic, with my angel as the only good thing you see in it. That one night was all you had. Imagine that night for the next five seconds and bless her for the gift she gave you. Then, I will let go, and you will run from my sight. If you don't, you will see why me choking you is a mercy, and you'll under-stand my real wrath. Do you understand?"

Creep nods as much as he can beneath the grip and William counts.

"One..."

I wring my hands, eyes bouncing between William and Damen.

"Two..."

Damen's eye turn to mine and I feel the fear in him. A deep part in me is exhilarated by William's aggression and the terror it brought Damen, but there isn't enough time for me to examine that quick thought.

"Three..."

Damen's face is nearly another color and I wonder if he'll pass out before the countdown concludes.

"Four..."

I swear William holds onto the second between four and five longer than he should.

"Five..."

William lets go and Damen falls to the floor, gasping and hoarse. He spends several seconds there, unable to catch his breath.

"What did I say?" William cautions, watching Damen's red face.

Damen looks up and gets to his feet, ready to run. He sees me fully and his eyes immediately fall to my growing baby bump. My hand falls to it protectively and I step back behind William, gripping the back of his shirt.

"Is that mine?" he asks in disbelief, voice cracking.

"Only in my worst nightmares." William answers with venom. "Now, what did I tell you would happen if you didn't run?"

Damen stumbles backward out of the elevator and

out of the apartment building as quickly as he can manage. William takes a deep breath and offers me his hand. I take it and we quickly walk out, passing a few whispering onlookers. Thankfully, it seemed like no one has called the police.

We reach the end of the block in silence, his hands shaking in mine, and William pulls me into the community parking garage.

"I need a moment," he says and takes a deep breath.

I pull our conjoined hands up to my chest and lay it above my heart. "I'm here. It's you and me. Everything is okay."

He nods and backs me up until I'm leaning against the side of the wall. His head drops to my forehead and he closes his eyes.

"Me and the baby are safe," I assure him.

"I know. I know. He just...He was horrible to you when you used to work together, then seeing he was the one you called and touched, even though I know I asked you to pick someone and he fit the description... it hurt that he got to do that with you, be with you, before I did. I hate him. I don't trust him. I don't want him anywhere near our baby," William explains, and my heart hurts. I haven't thought about it from his perspective, nor had I understood that it would hurt him.

"I don't want him. He was a means to an end.

Someone that I know would have used me, so I didn't feel bad using him. We'll never see him again," I say as evenly as I can, hoping to calm him. My hands reach for his hair and I caress him lightly.

"But he knows where we live," he says, voice elevated with concern. He reminds me of a pacing cat in this moment, tail twirling erratically in the air knowing there was an enemy close by.

"Not for long. We are going to move into the house your parents left you. We can leave within the month." It's a split-second decision, but we have another option that I know will soothe him and I didn't hesitate to use it.

"Really?" His voice lifts and I feel my eyes water in response. I love this man so much.

"Really. I figured we'd eventually move there anyway and I don't mind going early and setting it up for the baby. No one knows the address but us, he can't come back," I assure him.

"Good," he says in relief.

"William, can I ask you something?"

He nods into my neck. We stand here in the dark of the garage, holding onto each other. My stomach growls quietly and I hope he doesn't hear it. I don't want to rush him.

"The bad dreams you've been having...when you mentioned nightmares in the elevator, were you joking or do you dream that this baby isn't yours?"

He looks me in the eyes and bites his lip, hesitating. I know immediately this is his nightmare.

"Yes, my angel, some of them are about him. I know it's not true; it's impossible. But having you now —you are so important to me—makes me scared of losing you and the baby."

"That will never happen, my ghost. You never left me and I will never leave you."

His lips kiss mine tenderly, soft caresses that speak of how much he loves me, cherishes me, protects me. I love when we are rough together, desperate and needy, but in quiet moments like this I feel an intimacy I've never had before. I am cherished, treasured, and the feeling is mutual.

After a few minutes he pulls away and we continue on to the restaurant. At home, I remind him how much he rules my body and soul.

CHAPTER 16
FATHER

Today, I have to face my dad again. I'm still upset at my mom for bringing him back into the picture and telling him about our daughter, but I know that she had only hoped he'd be happy to be a grandfather. Honestly, I'm surprised she lasted as long as she did before calling. Mom has never been the kind of person to give up hope on someone, which is why she stayed married to him for so long even though no one was happy. I, on the other hand, lost that hope in my dad years ago.

Now he has the opportunity to inflict more emotional pain on me and I can't let him. I have a baby to protect. Part of me doesn't want to see him at all, to not go to the coffee shop and be a no-show. I purposefully picked the coffee shop I didn't like for our little reunion rather than my favorite one near my old job because I don't want him to ruin it. I don't have any good or precious memories at this chosen location, so if this goes badly it won't stain my usual coffee trips. As much as I don't want to go, I owe it to my mom to see him. I'll keep it brief and then never see him again. I'll make sure he is not invited to any baby event, no matter what Mom says.

"Emily," William says, sitting on our bed. We're moving next week, so there are boxes piled everywhere. He looks beautiful, as usual. He's wearing a black sweater with black pants, a leather belt with a gold belt buckle, and shiny shoes. Taking him shopping has been such a turn-on. He has a distinct style. I call it the "rich academic model" look.

"Yes, William?" I ask as I change my shirt for the twelfth time. Already, none of my clothes fit right. We've purchased a few maternity items, but I still struggle. I definitely need to redo my whole wardrobe.

"There is something about your Dad that I haven't told you."

This makes me pause, hands still up and face buried in fabric. "What is it?" I ask between the pleats of fabric. I pull it off and stand in my bra.

"I thought you'd never need to see him again, and I knew it would only hurt you to know this. And even though he is asking to meet you, I don't think you should go. I still hesitate to tell you, but it's dangerous and it would be worse if I didn't." He says all of this quickly, in one breath, and I blink for several moments, not understanding what he could know that I don't already.

"What do you mean? You think my dad is dangerous? I mean, he was an asshole, but he never laid a hand on me or Mom. What did you see when you'd ghost-visit him? Did he hit his other family?"

He's already told me about my half-sister, what else could there be?

"He is dangerous even without physical violence," William tells me.

"Is he a criminal?" I ask. Maybe his associates are the ones that are dangerous or he does other kinds of crime, like identity theft. I barely heard anything about his job, but if it were crime related, I wouldn't be surprised.

"He...this is hard to say." He gets up from the bed, pacing across our bedroom.

"You are scaring me, William."

I've never seen him be hesitant with his words. As far as I know, he hasn't ever lied to me. There would be no reason to. Yet, here we are. What could he have seen on those ghostly visits to my dad that he was scared to say aloud?

"I have a theory about why my spirit latched onto you when I died," he said instead, surprising me.

"What is it?" I prod, not liking the subject switch.

"I think you were the closest energy-focused being

near my death. My soul gripped yours because you absorb energy too."

My eyes crinkle and I say, "But, I'm not an energy being. I don't do what you do."

"Not exactly, but you are related to one."

"My dad was an incubus, too?" I'm horrified at the thought, but then pause for a millisecond realizing that was a judgment on my soon-to-be husband and the powers our daughter will likely have. I twirl my engagement ring around my finger, my eyes pleading for William to explain more.

"No, he was..." William paused, swallowing. "He was the energy vampire that murdered me and my parents."

I sit down with a thump on the bed, without words. I'm not even wearing pants yet. My arms close around myself and my stomach subconsciously.

William said he didn't know who the killer was, but he had known this whole time. He couldn't bear to say it because it involved me.

"How can you be with me? My family did this to you?" My voice cracks. The tears stream down my face and I hiccup. My breathing comes in fast and I cover my face with my hands, pulling my knees to my chest. How could my dad be responsible for his suffering?

William pulls me into his arms, cradling me as I cry. I mumble for some time, not sure how to process or handle this flood of information coming and coming in my life. His hands brush my hair, my back, in soothing strokes.

"This says nothing about you, Emily. You are not your father," William tells me in a soft voice. I don't believe him.

"He hurt you, your family, he hurt my mom, me—he is a monster. I'm a monster."

"No, Emily, you are not a monster."

He shushes me, rocking me and petting my hair. When I've settled, if you could call "settled" quietly staring at his chest and shivering–he asks, "What do you know of energy vampires?"

"Nothing but what I've seen on TV, which makes them look like funny guys that bother you at work and make you bored. Or people with a shitty regard for boundaries."

"True energy vampires are chosen for their penchant for pain, not for making a bad workplace environment," William tries to kid. "His power came as a manifestation of his desire to cause pain. Now, that mission makes him slow to age and craving to hurt more people so he can feed on them. You are his daughter, part energy vampire. You could have some of his powers for being related to him, but it isn't the same as someone that was chosen or manifested as an energy vampire. You would have more ability to control it than he ever would have, but he still had those choices before he fully ascended. He chose his path by devoting years to pain. Whatever parts of him that are dormant in you, if they manifest completely, you'll have a choice too."

My eyes are red and itchy by the time I release all the pent up emotion in my chest. I reach one hand to my lower stomach, pressing against where I knew I was bringing a new generation into the world. I have to protect my baby, our daughter. I have to protect my fiancé. I cannot be my father.

I ask a question I am scared to voice, "Is this why I've always been alone? Are people scared to be around me?"

"It's possible. It never seemed like people hated you. You didn't chase them away. But there is an otherness to you in the way you hold your energy that some people may subconsciously feel. I felt it. It brought me to you rather than scaring me away."

My heart aches, conflict hitting me like lightning strikes. In some ways, this is the answer I always needed. In others, I am enraged. Anger, acceptance, understanding, betrayal, it all courses through me. A thought strikes me that gives me profound guilt and I ask William before I lose the courage, "I'm so upset he did this to you, but I also feel glad that it brought us together. Does it make me a horrible person for thinking that?" I hold my breath and hope he under-stands it, or feels it in some way too, because this is so much. He and our daughter are the only good in this situation and I have to see it, and celebrate it.

"No, Emily. I've thought the same thing. I would never have wanted this to happen or for my parents to die, but it brought us together, it brought me my own family, and I think my parents would have chosen that for me, too. I've had years to come to terms with this, to grow my feelings for you while knowing the whole truth. I'm sorry to suddenly share all of this with you." His voice is grave, low and shaky.

"Why are you telling me now? I'm upset you kept this from me, but I understand how hard it must have been too. What made you change your mind?" I almost wish I didn't know, that this secret was kept because it's too cruel, too fucked up, and I want it gone. I'm making a baby with the genes of a murderer. I carry that in me.

"He could try to feed on you because of the baby. Succubi...they are like a drug to energy vampires. Succubi hold energy that is converted from passion, lust, creation, as you now know. It is a high to most energy consuming creations. I don't know if he'll be able to tell that you are pregnant with a succubus or not. If he knew, I'm concerned he'll try and kidnap you." William grips my forearms, running his thumb along my inner arm in an anxious motion. His greatest fear is me and the baby getting hurt. I've already seen how that fear drives him.

"This is a lot to process," I say meekly. "I really wish you didn't wait until the last fucking minute to tell me this." I'm angry, understanding, and defeated all at once. A thought pricks behind my eyes and my heart seizes. It's not just my baby he would want, or even just me that he would want to damage again. He already murdered William and his family once. What is there to stop him from doing it again?

"I know, it was wrong of me to keep this from you. I'm so sorry. I was so worried about protecting your feelings. I know how hard it was for you growing up feeling isolated. I was so focused on that pain that I didn't realize how not knowing was endangering you even more."

I can tell he is genuinely sorry and had my feelings at heart, but this shouldn't have happened.

"Do you promise you won't keep anything else from me again? I'm giving my genes, his partial genes, down to our daughter, and knowing all that could mean for her is important. Anything else huge like that, I have to know." I'm serious about this, but part of me needs to add a joke to it too. "Except if you think I look ugly in my maternity clothes. Don't ever tell me that."

I feel like I'm going through the stages of grief, pinballing back and forth between denial, anger, and disbelief in particular.

"I'm going to reschedule with him. I still think I

should see him; I think I need that closure. But we'll come up with a better plan. He says he is in town all week, let me move this by a few days and we'll figure it out, okay?" I lift my eyes to his and hold my breath. This is dangerous for all of us now. Does he understand why I don't want to just walk away?

"Okay," he replies after a breath. "I don't like it, but I understand. We'll make a plan to make sure you are safe. And if he says no to rescheduling?"

"Then you have what you want and I won't see him. But knowing what you've told me, I think he does want to see me and will reschedule just to get another hit of the pain he inflicted on me and mom."

"I think you are right," William admits and I see how it pains him.

I get up and sit on his lap, pulling his head to my breasts and holding him close. We take a few minutes to center ourselves before we move on in the only way we can, together.

CHAPTER 17
MURDERER

Last week, I thought I was a human. It turns out, they are my prey.

"I almost didn't recognize you," my murderous father comments as I sit down.

"That doesn't surprise me. You haven't seen me in decades." He will get no mercy from me. No forgiveness, no leeway. He is a monster and I will close him out of my life from this moment further.

I cross my arms and fuel all my hate into my stare. I hated him before, but now he is dead to me. This meeting is to make it clear that he will never be allowed in my life or with my children. William is close by, he walked into the cafe earlier and sat across the room, blending in as a customer. Though I can pick him out easily—I always will be able to. I'm wearing a deep blue sweater on top of my usual leggings and tank top with running shoes strapped to my feet.

"There are a lot of reasons why I couldn't stay, Emily. When you are older, you will understand," he said patronizingly. He looks older than I remember. His black, thick curly hair has long silver strands in it and his bushy eyebrows seem thicker than they did in my mind's eye. His nostrils are the same shape as mine, too wide to be called small but not wide enough to be called big. We have other similarities, but I'm not willing to see them in the face of my love's murderer.

"I understand perfectly well. You are an energy vampire and a murderer. You needed a new victim and mom was spent." There is no point in pretending I don't know. Transparency is going to happen in our relationship for once.

His grin stills and his eyes narrow as he reassesses me. If he is surprised I know, he doesn't say so, but he seems to be considering me differently.

"I should have stayed longer to feed on you," he comments as if he is talking about a much simpler matter than eating the painful emotions of his family.

Instead of responding, I raise my eyebrow like a villain in a fantasy series, showing more confidence than I truly feel.

"There is something different about you," he says, looking me up and down.

Despite knowing I am part energy vampire for only

a few days, it makes certain moments in my life a lot more clear. This revelation should have hurt, and in a lot of ways it does, but in a way it also empowers me. It brought me William and set him free. He would have stayed dead if it weren't for my history and my willingness to work with the energy between us.

My ghost is my addiction for an entirely different reason than the high my father would experience in killing him and his parents. I am not my father. I will not use what I am to hurt people.

My father sniffs the air in front of me, pushing his coffee cup to the side. When he turns to look at my fiancé, William is already staring back at him.

"What a delicious hypocrite you turned out to be, Emily, with your all-you-can-eat buffet," my father says, incorrectly assuming I am also feeding on an incubus to get high.

I cackle and snort, finding too much humor in what a horrible man my father has turned out to be.

"You are a horrible person," I start. "I didn't understand why you couldn't love me in the way I needed, but now that I know that reason, I have no need for you."

He doesn't care to respond at first, just takes a sip of his coffee. I'm about to demand his response when he chimes in, "Do you want to learn how to get the most out of him?"

I gasp. Seriously, he wants to teach me how to

murder someone he already murdered and doesn't even remember? I stand, pulling my bag over my shoulder and pointing at him to punctuate my thoughts.

"You will not speak to me, see me, or come back to my city ever again. You will lose Mom's number, never get near my husband, and you will never set eyes on my child."

"Is that all?" Dad drawls, seeming not to care nor intending to follow my demands.

"Don't talk to Keira or her mom ever again," I add. If he hasn't already left them, he should now.

To this, his eyes widen.

"Yeah, I know about everything Dad."

"I sincerely doubt that, darling." The term of endearment lays like ash in my mind.

"Goodbye, Dad. You are not invited to the wedding."

William stands and walks toward me. He places his hand on my back and we begin to walk out together. My father sniffs the air again as we do, a big-ole whiff with a roll up into his eye sockets. William cringes, eyes blinking as he looses a breath. I realize too late that my father is using his supernatural senses to taste my lover's energy. Anger boils in my veins. I stop and turn, grabbing a fist full of his hair. I pull, ripping his head down before he can counter.

"You"—I snarl into his face—"will never hurt another succubus or incubus again."

An unexpected strength pulses through me when fear enters his eyes. I let him go before giving into my impulse to bang his head on the table and watch his nose go bloody.

Inhaling, I feel a strength grow in me and realize what is happening. I was feeding on my father and his fear tastes like sweet revenge.

Releasing him, I look down into the eyes of the person whose love I wanted more than anything else as a child. Now I understand I never needed it in the first place.

I vow to protect William and those like him from people like my father. I don't know how yet, but that has never stopped me before.

CHAPTER 18
TRAP MEET PREY

Having him see and smell William was part one of the plan. My love would be bait. With my connection to my father, killing William would cause me great pain while also giving Dad a high from both angles. It was too delicious of a travesty for an energy vampire to ignore. Not that I would ever let him succeed.

The rest of the plan would not be so easy, especially because I haven't told William yet. It's only been two days since we saw my dad, but I know he isn't gone. Not after what he found out. He is hovering nearby; I know he must be. William hasn't said anything, but I see him looking behind us when we walk or checking out the window throughout the day. I haven't asked if he feels him near in that way he can sense all energy around him, or if he is just worried and scared after seeing his murderer again.

"Thank you Rosie, I appreciate this more than you know." I smile at her, so grateful for someone else in this new world of mine to talk to with honesty.

"Thank you for trusting me, Emily. If your dad is as bad as you say, he'll show his true colors, and then the problem will be handled. If he doesn't, then maybe he has changed."

"I don't think that will be the case. I wish I could say I am hopeful, but I'm not." I shake my head and touch my stomach again protectively. It's a habitual gesture now.

"In either case, your conscience is clear. This is a contingency. If what you think comes about, you are doing a favor to the community by taking him out. Not all energy vampires are murderers, but those that are must be stopped."

I nod my head solemnly and hold up the bag she gave me. "Thank you for the gift."

"Of course. I'm so happy to see you again. And knowing now that William was from a long line of succubi makes a lot of sense. These goodies will help with the pregnancy." She smiles and touches her heart crystal pendant. I can only imagine there are a lot of sex toys in this gift bag.

"I'm so glad I met you, Rosie. If there is anything I

can do to help you in return, don't hesitate to call me," I tell my new friend.

"I won't. We'll talk after this is settled. Don't worry, you'll all be okay."

As I walk out of the shop, I pray I've made the right decisions and that my soul won't be too tainted for it.

"ARE YOU SURE YOU WANT TO GO OUT TONIGHT?" WILLIAM asks me as he zips up my dress. I cannot reach behind me comfortably anymore and appreciate the help getting into my clothing, especially in this sexy number I've never worn. I had picked it up with the intention to look very fuckable while pregnant.

If his lingering eyes are any indication, I believe I have succeeded. It is the tightest little black dress I've worn since becoming pregnant, or ever now that I think about it. It's incredibly uncomfortable. It pushes up my breasts so much that they are practically all out there, now swollen and nearly two sizes bigger, and it emphasizes my bump so that I look *very* pregnant.

His hands roam my body in appreciation.

"I can think of several," he leans down and kisses each breast, "reasons to stay home tonight."

"There is always one *big* reason to stay home," I reply and cup the front of his pants. I let him go with a gentle squeeze, wiggle out of his grasp, and pat him on the shoulder as I pass. "But we've got a reservation and I've got a surprise for you." Our should-we-leave-should-we-not routine has become an increasingly common one. Often, when we do leave, we end up fooling around in the parking lot too.

"I love surprises," William says as he watches my ass leave our bedroom.

Our new home is a lot bigger. Honestly, there is enough for three families to fit comfortably. We don't need it, but it is safer.

I finish getting ready, William helps me get into my shoes, and we get on the way. I'm so glad William has learned how to drive in the past few months. I hate driving with my growing bump.

We arrive on a darkened street and turn off the ignition. William opens my door and extends his hand to help me out. I point to our destination: A little restaurant with candles littering the window and a trail of them up the sidewalk to the door. It's a twinkling beauty in the night and I stop and hope that my dad has changed so that we can enjoy our date uninterrupted.

"Is this my surprise?" William asks as we walk toward it. A car drives down the street and turns at the end, parking near a closed bookstore. A chill overtakes me when I glance at it, and not the kind I like. I look back to William and smile through my discomfort. He pushes my long hair over one shoulder and kisses my bare skin.

"You alright?" William asks me, leaning into my neck and taking in a deep breath through his nose. I feel his head lift up to stare behind me.

"Of course," I say. "Let's go in. We have the place to ourselves, all night."

He follows me in with a grin, hand laying gently on my lower back. The receptionist greets us and shows us to our table in the center of the dimly lit room. Her long black hair reaches her mid-back, swaying as she walks.

"Your server will be with you shortly, dears. Have a lovely evening, and happy anniversary," she says and walks away without hearing my thanks.

"It's our anniversary?" William asks with a chuckle. "What anniversary?"

I survey the setup: A large table more suitable for seating six rather than two, candles and low lighting. The other tables have been cleared to the sides so we have more space around us—it was just what I asked for.

"It is actually, of sorts. This month it will be twenty-two years since we met." Which also means the anniversary of his family's murder, but that isn't what I want to focus on.

"Hmm…" William says. "I'll have to get you a present."

He turns my chair so it faces him and bends down before me.

"What are you doing?" I shush him, this was not *yet* the time for a show.

"Relax, angel," he says and reaches for my feet. He pulls them in his lap, rearranging his chair so we were both comfortable at the new angle.

"You say we are alone in here?" he asks, petting my swollen ankles and rubbing lightly. One hand takes my left ankle up, kissing it once before unstrapping the heel.

"Yes, Rosie knows the owner. No one but us will be dining tonight," I tell him, an icy thrill shooting up my leg at his touch.

The server comes over and pauses mid-sentence, seeing William slowly pulling one foot out of my strappy heels. He makes it look like a deeply sensual act, lifting the heel slowly while running his other hand down my ankle and up my calf. He reaches to do the other foot and raises an eyebrow at the stunned server.

The server catches himself and blinks, pulling up his notepad to start over and get our order. William interrupts him, "Bring us whatever the chef likes to cook the most and two waters. Thank you."

"Right. Good choice, sir." He bows and quickly rushes away.

"You've scared the boy," I say with a pout.

"He wants to fuck me while you watch," William comments and delicately lowers my second foot to the floor.

"Ah, smelled some arousal on him did you?" I'm constantly amazed by what he can pick up from people.

He pushes his chair back and drops again to his knees. This time, he doesn't get back up. Instead, kisses are trailed up from my feet, calves, to my thighs. He pushes my skin-tight dress up slowly until I'm sitting in my thong with my dress pinched up to my waist.

"I smell more than just *his* arousal," he whispers between my legs. His kisses slow and his tongue flicks out, snaking closer and closer to my mound. I whimper at his familiar cold.

"He could come back at any moment," I whisper as my head falls back against the chair, already giving in.

"Good," William says, and his mouth finds my underwear. He keeps it on, kissing me through the fabric. He makes out with my underwear as if it were my mouth, lapping me and swirling his tongue as if it sought mine.

I whimper again and move my hips up and down

against his face. He continues to kiss me, hands holding my thighs on his shoulders.

My moan fills the quiet space. I gasp and cover my mouth, trying to quiet down.

William looks up and moves his mouth enough to speak, "Don't you dare."

I quiver beneath him.

"Be a good girl and I'll let you come on my face. No holding back. Be loud, my baby girl."

"Yes," I say and shake, "I'll be good."

"Good," he says with a cold breath on my cunt. I squirm and he finally pulls back my soaking under-wear. His mouth reaches for my clit and sucks force-fully. I come like a force of lightning, shaking and moaning as I punt up on his face, feeling the friction of his jaw against my center as his mouth unrelentingly sucks.

I attempt to calm myself as William pulls away and repositions my ruined underwear and wrinkling dress. He helps me lift my hips so it can cover my body again. He calmly sits back into his chair as if nothing happened. He is wiping my pussy juices off his face with the restaurant's linen napkin when the server comes around the corner holding two glasses of water.

"Great timing, I'm parched," William comments to the man. The server blushes a deep red, not looking either of us in the eye, and leaves the glasses.

I smile into my glass as I take a sip. "Enjoy your

feeding on us?" I ask my fiancé, knowing he took from both me and the arousal of the server who obviously listened nearby.

"Delicious. Getting full before the food is even here," he says with a wink.

"Don't get full before dessert," I tell him. For what I have planned, he needs his appetite.

CHAPTER 19
BETRAYAL

While I'm finishing up my steak, the receptionist pops into the room. She stays on the edge and gives me a thumbs up.

"What's going on?" William asks, looking up and seeing the exchange.

"I have ulterior motives with this anniversary visit," I tell him, grimacing.

"I figured since your father has been following us."

"And when were you going to tell me that?" I demand.

"When were you going to tell me that you also noticed? Because that's been obvious," he counters.

"Well...right now. It's part of the plan," I say awkwardly.

"Enlighten me on the plan," he says and reaches for my napkin, his laying spoiled on the table.

"The receptionist is a vampire slayer," I start, to which William raises his brows, eyes widening in surprise. I quickly add, "Not to kill him, but to trap him."

He loosens a breath as if in relief and I don't understand. I just said I wasn't going to kill his murderer, wouldn't he want me to?

He pulls my chair to him and gently holds my face, thumb grazing my lips. "I would never want you to have to make that choice. Now tell me the rest, how is this going to work?"

I take a deep breath and smile at the man who treats me with such kindness and respect. "Since Dad followed us, there are a few ways to get into the building. She signaled that he is coming closer now and looking around. We're going to...get intimate and see if he tries to feed on us. If he does try to do so and hurt us, we'll be a distraction while the slayer can overtake him and bring him to a facility where he won't be able to feed anymore. He'll slowly waste away there, not able to hurt anyone else."

His thumbs release my jaw and stroke down my neck to my collarbone.

"We're the bait?" William asks, something unrecognizable flashing across his eyes.

"No, we're the trap," I say. It's only slightly different, but it's more empowering. No father should be willing to do this, not only to watch his daughter have sex, but to take enjoyment in it? If he isn't corrupt, he will leave before it's too late. Coming here was his choice no matter I did, I feel absolved in that way.

"I'd be trapped with you any day," he says and pulls me into his lap. With my bump it's a little less comfortable to be on top, but when he kneads my thighs and sucks on my neck, I forget a lot of things that initially make me uncomfortable.

"Do you forgive me?" I ask in a husky tone when he pulls away from the marks he's claimed on my neck.

"You should have told me you were planning something. You put us all in danger by keeping it a secret," he says with a frown. "But I did the same by not telling you who he was earlier, so I can't be one to judge. Let's get him out of our life and start clean, with no more lies or half truths. Agreed?"

I rub myself against his hard length, pushing my breasts into his face, and tell him yes.

"Will you protect me? Please, protect me and our baby," I moan into him, rocking my hips up and back. His hands pull up the edges of my slim dress to my hips, giving me more space and freeing my ass for him to grab.

He growls into my lips. "I'm so turned on and so angry with you at the same time."

"Mutual," I breathe and buck again. We could have

made a plan sooner if I knew what had really happened. But as it was, I didn't trust him to let me be part of the bait with him. He would have likely tried to do this on his own, and I wouldn't have let him.

"My angel, acting like a devil," he says, voice gravely and wanting.

I lean into him, working to forget all that has happened. Focusing on us, our love, the life we are building. Part of me still knows danger is near, but I have my protector with me.

"Love me, protect me," I pant.

"Always," he prays to me, reaching behind me for the zipper of my dress. He lifts me to pull the dress off, leaving me in my drenched thong and painful push-up bra. The server rushes in to take the plates, almost dropping them in his rush to leave the room. I stop breathing for a moment before relaxing when I hear his feet trail away.

"I take it the staff knows why we are here, what we are doing," William comments, keeping his eyes on me. He admires my body, caressing my bump and humming in appreciation as he looks at my spilling breasts.

"They know this is a trap for an energy vampire, they are all acquaintances of Rosie." That woman knows everyone.

"Good, then it won't matter when I make you scream my name."

He lifts me up and lays me down on the table like a meal. I reach down and hold my bump before leaning back, bracing my body on my elbows.

"And if I don't scream?" I question him, even though I know it's going to happen one hundred percent.

He smiles, calling my bluff. "You'll scream for me."

"You are awfully confident for someone that was a virgin until four months ago," I say softly, goading him.

"Must be the demon in me," he purrs and pulls my legs so that he sits between them. I hum my approval at the tent in his pants pressing against me.

A knock sounds behind us. I whisper, "He's in the building."

"If he wants to take me again, he'll have to pull me from his daughter's pussy," William tells me huskily.

That shouldn't turn me on as much as it does, but my body doesn't listen to my mind.

He undoes his belt and the sound is Pavlovian. My mouth waters and my cunt is ready.

"Fuck me now," I command my ghost.

He unleashes his layered cold length into me and I'm already close. He pounds into me like the demon he is. We aren't slow, loving, or careful as passion erupts between our two forces: His identity as a sex demon and mine as a newly aware energy vampire.

There is so much I don't know and don't even care

to understand about who I am. Yet, I will admit that knowing I am also a creature helps me see the freedom we were meant to have together.

Our bodies writhe together on the table that I specifically asked to be this size. If the staff thought the request for a large round table was strange when I asked, they certainly understand the need now. We stay like this, unrestrained, for several long minutes before I start to feel my energy leave me. It's different than William's feeds where he takes from our bodies slowly and in drips, savoring. My father seems to have no such desire to make it a long, drawn-out experience. He is taking, taking, taking as quickly as he can. He devours his high, as if he is taking with the intent to devour until our death.

My attention is waning and I find it hard to catch my breath. William slows and I know he feels it too. He pulls my body up, brow to brow, and kisses me gently. I whimper into him, and he blows his cool air on my face to help me calm down.

"It's almost over, angel. We're okay," he tells me. I nod against him and his pelvis rocks slowly into mine. I'm safe. I'm safe. We only have to hold out a little while longer. We hired a slayer, we are a trap, we just have to keep holding a murderer's attention.

I find I can't pull away, taking solace in what could be our combined last breaths. I didn't want to be right about my father, but the truth is clear. He planned to suck me, my baby, and my fiancé for all the energy we have. He's willing to kill his kin, his granddaughter and son-in-law—twice, not that he knew it—for the high of it. He doesn't just want to feed on us, he's here to kill. I try to speak again, but my words get stuck in my throat. If I hadn't asked for help, this would be the end, and I've only just now started to live.

"It's okay," William whispers in my ear. "You're safe. We have friends here. Nothing will happen to you or Cassandra."

"Cassandra?" I ask. We have been debating our daughter's name all month and he said he didn't like my number one choice.

"It's grown on me," he tells me and kisses my brow.

Tears leak from my eyes and my arms tighten around his back.

"I love you," I tell him, realizing we so rarely say it aloud.

"I love you too, my angel," he replies.

His subtle rocking continues, the ridges of his cock rubbing along my walls in the delicious way they always do. We barely move, yet I feel so much. At the edge of the table with him standing between my legs, shirt off and pants pooled at his feet, I know whenever we are connected, no matter the circumstance, I am home.

The word love feels too simple, too inconsequential, for the experience we have. To have found me when he was a ghost, our growing bond spanning years of trust, to the beginnings of magic, and now life that binds us together. We used what we felt for each other; our bodies, the conduit to express it, to bring him across planes of existence...love is not enough for us. It cannot describe the life we have brewing between us or the beating of our simple hearts.

There's a loud rush in my veins, and I don't realize the gradual buildup of my orgasm until I come apart on him.

"William," I call into his shoulder, gripping him tightly. The sound of me screaming his name puts him over and he releases into me. We're both weak, being fed on with evil intent, and his low groan sounds almost pained.

William tumbles back into the chair, me on top of him. We're both sweaty, cold, and pale. I move up and down on his slackening piece, feeling his seed slip in and out of me, enjoying the slickness. My heartbeat slows and I shiver. Resting my head on his shoulder, I slow down and grow contended and tired. We're about to fall asleep on each other, depleted, when a crash sounds behind us.

I blearily look up and William mumbles. In front of me, the receptionist has my dad tied up like a hog. He is seething on the floor, yelling for his release, spitting and shaking. His eyes are red, body glowing in an otherworldly purple with the energy he stole from us. The receptionist takes out a long syringe that had been cuffed beneath her pant leg and exposes the needle. She has one knee pushed down on my father's chest with one hand bracing his head to the side. She pushes the plunger down into his neck and whatever is in the needle hits its mark. He goes still.

The receptionist nods her head at me and says our server will be back with water and a second round of food to help us regain strength. She stashes the syringe and pulls on the binding holding my dad, dragging the man I once thought of as family behind her.

My eyes follow her and I manage a question before she departs, "Where will you take him?" All I know is that he will be kept from harming others, but I don't know how.

"An enclosed cell at one of my facilities. It's coated in magic that keeps anyone inside from feeding or being fed on," the receptionist says. "We have a monitoring system to make sure he doesn't escape while his power weakens. If you ever want to speak or visit him, just let Rosie know and she'll get us in touch."

I nod, clutching to William's neck. The receptionist looks down at my body and I remember she has a full view of my ass from this angle. William tells her our thanks, his voice barely carrying across the space.

We both slump when my father is pulled out of the building and into the van waiting outside. It drives away with a screech. I pull myself off of him and lay on the floor. He joins me and we lay together on the dark carpet.

The server does indeed come in, pausing when he spies our still obvious nudity.

"I brought mozzarella sticks and water. I thought carbs would be helpful. Should I bring ice cream instead? Or cookies?" he rambles, standing above us holding the waters and a plate of steaming fried and breaded cheese.

I can't help but giggle. The added oxygen to my system makes me dizzy and I laugh harder. William joins me, laughing louder than I've ever heard him. He lifts his body and hovers over mine, covering me and laughing into my neck.

We eventually accept the food, ice cream and cookies too, and get dressed. We finish our anniversary and head home. We sleep for nearly three days on and off, regaining our strength after near death, and move on in a safer world.

CHAPTER 20
AWAKENED

Despite knowing my dad would betray me, it still hurt to know he took the bait. It wasn't surprising, but it was disappointing. Also, really fucking weird that he didn't hesitate to watch his daughter have sex so he could feed on her and her fiancé's sexual energy.

It's been four days since I laid the trap, and I still felt exhausted getting out of bed. But I don't have time to waste. With what had happened, we called our OB-GYN to get her next available appointment to be sure everything is still progressing as usual. There is no data on what an energy vampire feeding on you could do to a pregnancy, so who knows if this could have hurt our daughter. William believes we'll be fine, but I need a little more assurance.

I turn to William's side of the bed and smile into

his chest. I'll never get used to having him physically with me. After so many years with him as a ghost, having him alive and here is still such a miracle. I hope I never become too complacent to feel the beautiful impossibility that is our relationship.

"We've got to get up," I tell him and slide my leg over his. He grumbles and pulls me closer.

We don't get up until about an hour before the appointment and scramble to get dressed and eat fast food on the way. Dr. Bones gives me and the baby a clean bill of health with a very funny prescription to have more sex to reinvigorate our cells with energy again, and we go on our way. Now that I think about it, the past four days are the longest we've been without sex since I got pregnant.

"Doctor's orders," William whispers to me as he leans me against the wall of our shower after we arrive back at home. I gladly take my medicine and plan a second dose later.

"I need to tell her that he's gone," I say during dinner. We are sitting at the smaller dining table that I think is technically supposed to be a breakfast nook, but the main dining room is too big for just the two of us.

"Who? Your mom?" William asks.

"No, definitely not. She can never know she was only food to him. That would kill her." Who my Dad is and what he did to us has to remain a secret. After all she has been through, I can't let my mom know it was on purpose. She will never see my dad again, so the faster she can get closure, the better.

I pause to think before adding, "I meant Kiera. She could have felt the same loneliness I did. Or be using her powers without realizing it. I have to tell her what I know. It's the right thing to do, I've avoided thinking about and meeting her for months now and I think it's time."

"Then we'll find her and tell her. I agree. And it would be nice to let her know that she is an aunt, too. I can't pop over and see where she is right now since I'm not a ghost anymore, but I did learn enough that I think I could find her online."

I smile, my hand grazing over my swelling stomach. "Thank you. I can't imagine how hard all of this has been. You've had to change and adjust to so much. Growing up as a ghost, just watching me as the world changed around you, I can't imagine what that must have been like."

"I'm not going to pretend it isn't difficult, adjusting to having a body again and starting my life as an adult when I left it as a child, but I have you to help me through it."

"Life has so many milestones in it and many of

them you had to skip or see through my eyes. We'll keep doing that, we'll give you all the experiences you missed." A thought interrupts my brain and I feel guilt attach to me. I didn't just take my dad away from the world and my mother, I took him away from Keira. I never stopped to wonder...What if she wanted to make that decision for herself? Once I talk to her, I'll have to ask her if she would like Rosie and the receptionist's information so she can see or visit him.

"And with what happened with my dad last week? How did you feel seeing him?" I ask William, shaking away my worries for a moment. I'll meet Kiera and take it a step at a time.

"I am really fucking angry for myself, of course, but I'm mostly angry on your behalf. Wanting to kill me again didn't surprise me, but that he went after his daughter and granddaughter? That he had no qualms with killing a pregnant woman? I have no words to describe how despicable he is and I'm so glad he will never be in our lives again."

"Are you mad I didn't ask the slayer to kill him? And instead he is just incapacitated?" I look down into my plate hoping I didn't let him down.

He reaches for my hand across the table, gripping it. I look up at him with unshed tears.

"I would *never* ask you to kill. No matter what they did or who they are. If a time ever comes where it is required, I will kill for you, my angel."

I get up to sit on his lap and we hold each other until our hearts slow. When I release him, our hands join together on my growing stomach without thought. I look down at the swell and whisper to little Cassandra, "You will have a loving family, little sweetie, I promise you."

CHAPTER 21
BIRTH
FIVE MONTHS LATER

"This baby needs to come out of me," I whine and pout. I've heard that babies don't typically come on their due date, but if I'm the exception I will be very happy. While I have enjoyed a lot of my pregnancy, I'd be lying if I didn't say it's wearing on me. The past month of bed rest has not helped my mood.

William sits at the foot of the bed and picks up my swollen feet. I can't see my feet most of the time, let alone touch them. I sigh in relief with the simple touch.

"I've got you, my Emily. Don't worry. The baby will come soon."

He rubs my feet and moves up toward my calves, kneading my tense muscles. My relief quickly transforms into moans of sensual pleasure, feeling the stress release with his attentive ministrations and my body ignites again—as it always does.

"I read that certain activities can help induce labor," I say, bringing my hands to my own breasts. They are as swollen as the rest of me, aching and ready for a baby to nurture. I'm wearing a maternity satin sleep dress which helps me stay as cool and comfortable as possible.

"Hmm, really?" William asks, hands snaking up under the hem of my dress. I can't even remember the last time I wore pants. I sigh in relief when his thumb presses on my clit.

"Please make me feel good," I pray, leaning down on my pillow.

"Your ghost is here. I will make you feel good again."

He dives beneath my belly and peppers kisses along my thighs, biting and leaving his mark on me. I cry out with each suck and quiver when he finally reaches my sensitive cunt. With big lapping licks, he primes me until I'm begging for his seed again.

I've never been able to get enough of it. I want his come every day. Feeling his thick magic fluid is all that satisfies me.

"Give it to me," I demand again. "Hurry, please, please, please."

He holds back, pushing a finger and then three into my pussy. He is brutal about it, fucking me harder and harder with his hand until I'm no longer able to form words. In and out, in and out, in a punishing rhythm.

His slick fingers push in more, more, until he is adding his thumb, his palm, and his full hand to the wrist enters me. This isn't the first time he has done so in my pregnancy, but we have been careful to avoid it in the third trimester. Until today. I convulse around him as if possessed.

"Fuck, fuck, fuck," I repeat. I can't stop the orgasm that rips through me at the invasion of my body. I pulse around his hand and push up as he pushes in. I convulse with his hand in me, crying out my orgasm in a long wail.

Being pregnant with a succubus baby has been a very delicious trial. While it has drawbacks, like being horny twenty-four seven, it has opened me up to new creative positions and even new hobbies. As William likes to remind me: It is not just sexual energy, but creation energy, so the amount of DIYs I've made for the baby room and our house as I've been nesting has been insane. This house is not recognizable to what it used to be. We are in a happy, lived-in, creative home full of joy, patterns, and love. And our bedroom—and living room most of the time—seems to carry the mist of sex like a cloud.

"I'll get you ready for our baby, Emily. You'll be just

fine," William promises me. When he slowly pulls his hand from me, covered in my come, he massages my sides, opening me as fully as I can. It helps calm my nerves from his fist. He is so protective of me, giving me what I need. Well, I need his come, but first he massages every crevice of me, even dipping to the skin between my pussy and anus to rub and lubricate. He read in my baby book that daily massages could prevent me from ripping during birth.

My patience was over, however, the air of my orgasm already fading.

"Fuck me now," I command from our bed. To say I have been needy these last few weeks is an under-statement. I'm so glad I left my job because sex has pretty much replaced all of those working hours.

"My demanding angel," he whispers to me.

He keeps his pants and shirt on, muscles straggling against his shirt, and reaches for his fly. His thick bumpy girth of a cock springs free of his trousers and slaps beneath my stomach. For someone who has only been human for nine months, he is the perfect speci-men. He palms my sex again, cooling me down with his lower-than-normal body temperature. I grind against his palm and complain before he finally pulls back and gifts me with his cock.

Feeling him inside me? He brings me as much to life as I did him.

I pull my dress fully off while he stays clothed. He

holds my legs down, stretching me as he pushes through. A moan from deep in my chest escapes me.

"Yes, yes, yes," I hiss. I lean up on my elbows to see him in his button-down, blonde chest hair peeking out from the top two unbuttoned V of his chest.

"Mine," I snarl at him.

"Yours," he agrees with a satisfied smirk.

I smile at him as he pounds into me. I hold my pleasure at bay, shining it all through my eyes as we stare unblinking at each other, in a silent competition with him on who can stay quiet longer. He pounds me, jostling my full breasts, and my stomach hardens in a cramp.

I bite my lip when William tilts his pelvis up, so he does it again and again. I pant, fighting to keep my moans at bay, refusing to break my eye contact. The cramp pulses again and I massage my stomach, wincing before the pleasure distracts me again.

"You want me, Emily?" William asks, teasing me, thrusting with each word.

"I want your come, that's what I want," I say to him, needy. "I'm done waiting. Give it to me."

"Anything you wish, Emily," he replies, losing my silent dare, a groan exploding from his mouth that undoes me.

We come at the same time, moaning and shivering as he fills me with so much unending fluid that it leaks out of me. I finally collapse my head back on our soft pillows. I'm sticky and happy, just as I like to be, but I want more. When he releases me, I turn on my side and stick my hand between my legs. I have to arc on my side to do it and I barely reach. William takes off his remaining clothes and lays behind me, skin to skin, moving my hand and replacing it with his to help me reach my goal.

His hands dips into the wetness and then swirls it up over my clit. He pulls another orgasm out of me, slowly, and I bend, clenching with the mix of back pain and pleasure. He rubs me patiently, over my sensitive nub again and again. My stomach clenches again, hard as a rock, and I groan in pain.

"It's almost time, my Emily. It's okay, love. Stay with me, feel my hand."

I pant, reaching back to pull his head into my neck. He plants gentle kisses there and bites to distract the pain when another contraction forces itself free.

"Our baby is coming," I whisper, something I've realized in the past several minutes but was contended to ignore. I wanted this all day, all week even, but now I am faced with the reality. That fork in the road, that one decision that I was warned would change it all, is now coming into fruition.

"You're coming first," he promises me and rubs faster.

"Not again, not again, I can't." This is the only time it's ever been too much, too overwhelming, to keep being pleased. I had our juices, his and mine, all around me. In my cunt, swirled on my mound, rubbed between me in massage. I am a sticky, quivering mess of pleasure, and he unendingly wants to give me more. I'm sore, but I know that more is coming. I got my wish. I'm going to have my baby today, and I'm depleted of energy because she is taking it all from me, draining me, to get out into this world.

William is giving himself to us so we can be strong.

In answer, he leans into my neck, kissing along my shoulder and up to the shell of my ear.

"Unleash yourself, my angel. Use me, feed on me. Let me give you my strength."

I have only done it once, by accident when I met my father. I was unaware of that side of me for so long. Energy vampires get high on succubi and incubi; it's their favorite treat. Can I handle that temptation?

"What if I like it too much? What if I hurt you, or I can't stop?" I ask, scared.

His arms wrap around me, one scooping under to cover my heart and the other around my stomach. "You are not your father. You are a born energy vampire. You don't act on it, but it's a natural part of you. I trust you. I'll help you. You are weak. Your body is giving all that it can for our child. Our sex life has helped balance that, transferring energy to her to help her grow, but you are not a succubus. You aren't taking in my energy in the same way, and it's weakening you.

Use what was given to you to offset it, so that you can have more to bolster you in birth. It could be harder on you otherwise."

I think on his words, leaning as much as I can into his back.

"Okay," I say hesitantly. "How do you tap into your powers? What should I try?"

If he trusts me, and I trust him, then logically it should be okay. I'm not always good at logic, but my body is hurting and my baby is coming and I can't let emotion rule me now.

His arms run soothingly down my arms as he explains, "Take a deep breath and reach into the protectiveness in you. You don't feel the urge to feed like your father does. For you, it needs a purpose. When you fed briefly on your dad, it was to protect me from him. Think on that now. This feed is to protect you and to make birth easier for our baby. Imagine our child, what she needs, and take that from me. The instinct will be there."

I listen to him and close my eyes, focusing my thoughts inward. They wander, but I pull them back, imagining my little baby inside me. In response, Cassandra kicks me and repositions herself. My stomach stretches and moves in front of me. William laughs in my ear, hovering his hand over where Cassandra has settled her foot.

"I'm here, baby. Me and your daddy are here. We

can't wait to meet you." I stroke my stomach, closing my eyes again and focusing on our love as another contraction pulls on me. I feel into all that I feel for our future and the hopes I have for her and breathe. I inhale in and out for several minutes and then pause, realizing the air smells distinctly different, as if it's heavier. I imagine in my mind's eye the air as fog. With each inhale the fog gets pulled into my body. The pain lessens and I feel clearer; more alert than before. When I exhale, I imagine thin vapor, as if I took what fueled the fog into me to keep.

"You've got it, angel. It's working," I hear William's voice like a beacon, a bright light in my mind's eye, guiding me home. I inhale again and shiver, feeling a new thrill in me. I remember what William told me, that all my senses are conduits, and it feels like a perfect time to lean back into my sense of touch.

I pant and crane my head behind me to drag his lips to mine. His hands stop their soothing pattern and instead grip my hip, pulling my ass against him and arching my back. His cock rubs against me and I smile into his lip.

"Hungry for me?" I ask.

"Starved. But this is for you, angel. Let me feed you," he answers in a husky whisper.

His tongue swirls in mine, moving his free hand to separate my cheeks, pumping his head against the cluster of sensitive cells. I nod into his kiss, answering his silent question.

We have done anal a few times in the past. I preferred his come in my cunt then my ass, but feeling it leak from that small hole and slipping into my pussy? That was a different kind of delicacy and the pinch of pain and fullness would distract me from my growing contractions as I fed.

His hauntingly cold body surrounds our joining, cooling me as I start to cry. Tears run down my face as I feel the combination of pleasure and pain from all angles. His consistent rubbing of his come on my swollen lips, the head of his ribbed wide dick jammed behind me, and the contractions readying me to push. Each touch fuels me, giving me a thrill unlike anything I've had before.

William cries out behind me, coming again. My ass fills with more of his seed and I ride another contraction wave. They are coming closer together now. He bites my shoulder and whispers in my ear, "My beautiful Emily, the angel that saved me from death. You are stronger than you know. You can do this."

He stays in me as he grows limp, gently pushing. Even at half-mast, his layered cock stimulates me and I hum in delight at the combination of his rhythm, his cold come leaking between us, and the high of chasing his primal creation energy.

My sex drive, the naughty dreams, my constant

need for not just the act but for his seed, they all have given the needed life energy for our baby's birth. I did eat more, I did gain weight and grow to bring room for this child, but I never felt the cravings I had seen online or heard from the other students in our birthing class. All I've wanted was our pleasure, and that fed the growth of our child. And now, my fiancé is sharing with me the life energy he was given back. Not too much, but what I will need to keep me safe in birth, with a child I chose to bring into our family and save my love.

I understand now how tempting my future husband and his kind must be to energy vampires. I feel as if the universe is exploding in my heart and that each cell in my body is a big bang star—reaching out for more and more expanses to explore. Feeding on him is a solitary experience that anyone would want to experience, for creation and passion itself lives within him. But I am stronger than that want because he gave it to me freely, for our child, and I would never spoil that gift.

I smile as we mix pleasure and pain together, knowing me and William did our part.

He helps me release my hold on his energy and we cry together, relief and happiness commingling for this new chapter in our life.

We dress and he carries me to the car, buckling me

in before he gets in to drive me to the hospital. We call ahead and make sure our doctor is aware it's time.

William holds my hand as they get ready to take me to my room, kissing my knuckles, my ring, and tells me all will be okay.

I'm ready.

CHAPTER 22

TO HAVE, TO HAUNT
A YEAR AND A HALF LATER

While I have always wanted to be a mom, I've never imagined what my wedding will look like. For me, it isn't as important. But with William, I have actually wanted to dream about it. The moment we became pregnant, I started imagining how it would all come together. I wanted to wait until after our baby was born, as there were so many things to consider, and it is finally time. The dream I didn't know I wanted has started coming together in an intimate ceremony on our estate and then we will be off to the honeymoon of a Pinterest girl's dreams.

The orchestra signaling it's my turn fills the air. I take a centering breath and make my way toward the aisle. I did not wear white, it didn't feel right for me. Instead, my satin dress is a russet orange. It is long and breezy with thin straps on my delicate shoulders and a low back. My brown hair is styled in waves behind me, covering some of the long dip of exposed skin. We chose sunset for our ceremony so the temperature would be cooler and to symbolize our uniquely different worlds molding together.

My sister, Kiera, agreed to be my maid of honor, and was in a similar dress of pale blue. I haven't known my half-sister long, but I knew if I was going to have anyone up there with me, it would be the sister I have grown to love. We've connected a lot this year, at first bonding over the destruction of our father, then later as we grew to understand what it meant to be energy vampires. We did not manifest into one, we were born as one, and while the temptations are different, they are still there. It seems to ignite in me the moment I know of it, like when I felt my dad's fear, but Kiera has had the urges longer than me. I'm glad I'm not alone in this. I'll never have to be again.

I walk myself down the aisle. My Mom is sitting in the front row holding Cassandra. Starting a family helped me and my mother rekindle a tentative friendship. It will be put to the test while she watches Cassandra in our house for the week while on our honeymoon. Kiera will still be in town for a few days and she is also staying at the house, so at least for half of the time she will be there to help mom.

I wish that William could still visit people in the

blink of an eye like he could as a ghost so that he could check on our daughter, but he hasn't kept much of his ghost life except for his body running colder than average. Out of all that could have happened, I'm grateful he retained his incubus cock when he came back to life.

We have yet to see what Cassandra has inherited from both our powerful heritages. She probably won't show any signs for a few years. No matter what happens, or how her powers present themselves, she'll have the support of her family like William did. And a special school with otherworldly instructors and students that Rosie referred us to when it was time. Thankfully, we are years out from that.

Benches instead of seats line the aisle with baby's breath in bunches between them. There aren't many attendants since I didn't have many friends and William only recently came back to life. William has no family but me and our daughter. His parents didn't have any cousins or extended family for us to contact when he came back, only those that had been entrusted to watch his estate. The caretakers came as a courtesy, but we barely saw them at the house—that's just the nature of their species. They like the quiet more than anything.

I smile at William, walking toward him as the pink and orange sky slowly turns black. At the top of the aisle is my beautiful man. My spirit has been made whole. A tear spills from the corner of my eye even though I swore I would not cry. In my hands I hold a bushel of greenery and white roses, and Kiera reaches out to hold it as I reach him. William smiles softly at me, a tuft of his floppy brown hair falling in his face. He holds my hand, eyes full of love. He looks transformed with the sun behind him. For a moment, I imagine him as the shimmering spirit that grew up with me.

I still can't believe it sometimes. Our love story was not expected, but I would not change it for anything in the world. The years that have led up to this were hard and lonely, but William's constant shivers that kept me company are a fond memory in the gray.

I look at him and the tears gathered swell over. He leans forward and kisses beneath my eyes, removing the evidence of my tears. I giggle and pull him closer and he covers my lips with his.

"You were supposed to say I do first," the officiant reminds us with a cough.

We pull back, smiling, and turn back to him.

"We're ready," I tell him and he starts the predetermined ceremony William and I had agreed on. I barely hear a word of it, lost in his brown eyes, until we reach the prompt to say our vows.

"Emily, I came into your life under strange and painful circumstances. But in those moments, I found someone who grounded me as I sorted through what I needed. You didn't know it, but for so long in those early years I clung to you as we were in the grips of our shared aggressor," his voice chokes and I hold his hand tighter, giving him a watery smile.

"When I got to finally call you mine, the whole world shifted, and I saw in color. You became the woman that made me a man, and now a father and husband. I'll always love you for that, but also for so much more." He swallows and bites his lip, something I so rarely see him do. My heart stutters, not used to seeing him nervous. I mouth *I love you* and he continues with a smile, squeezing my hand back gratefully.

"You are strong, fierce, protective, and kind. You are loving, resilient, and unbroken even when beaten. You are a brave and thoughtful mother, giving and teaching in a way that will prepare her to honor herself and what she needs in a world that tries to take. I am lucky to know you, lucky to love you, and grateful to have been in your sphere even when I was out of reach, even when it was a tragedy to not touch you. You were mine and I was yours before we even had any hope to be so."

He adds one last line before letting my hand go to wipe his own tears, and I melt. "I'll love you mortally, eternally, and forever after."

I break from what I'm supposed to do again and

pull him into a hug. When I eventually let go, I nod to the officiant and say the lines I practiced in my head so many times the past few months.

"Love is something you do more than feel. In our good times and bad, you've shown your care through action. When there was nothing we could do but be in each other's presence, I knew what was brewing in us, but I convinced myself it was one-sided because I didn't think I was worthy of it." I say the words but my voice shakes. "When I gave our impossibility a chance, I knew I would never be able to turn back, and I was willing to put in that risk because the thought of never knowing was eating away at me. But life found a way, and we were willing to listen, giving our love a once-in-a-lifetime chance that no one would be able to accurately describe."

We're both crying again with smiles on our faces. I hear a sound from the guests and look to see Cassandra fighting to be let out of my mom's lap. I tell her it's okay and she lets go, our toddler ambling up the aisle and stopping between our legs. I bend down and pick her up, brushing a fluffy brown curl away from her green eyes. I tuck her into one side and hold William's hand with the other.

"Our love story is one filled with magic, hope, and chances. Every day, we'll be faced with the same choice, to continue on that journey or let the magic go.

I'll choose you and our magic every day and show you how much you mean to me and our daughter."

I sniffle and repeat back to him the sentiment he gave me, knowing they will leave a tattoo on my heart, "Mortally, eternally, and forever after, I'll choose you."

The officiant continues on with the rest of the program until we say *I do*, and William and I walk back down the aisle with Cassandra between us, together.

CHAPTER 23
HONEYMOON

This is a honeymoon I never thought I'd be able to afford. Like those cute Instagram models, I'm laying in my own private bungalow in the Maldives. It took several days just to reach the location. William spoiled us by getting the best flights and hotel accommodations in between connections. He took every opportunity he could to make love to me or show his affection. Being with an incubus is quite the experience and for the first time in a while, we are alone. Having Cassandra changed the dynamic of our relationship because now we can't have sex anywhere at any time and we have to practice a little more discretion. That is, when we are home. When Cassandra is at daycare, I'll admit we have sex in deserted public places often.

But it isn't just the sex, though, *wow*, that is an

experience. Ever since I opened up to my powers as an energy vampire, I understand how addictive incubus and succubus can be. I was hesitant at first, to taste the power that William offered me, but he has helped me understand that being what we are means a natural exchange between us. He has told me what taking energy from me is like during our intimate moments, and that he wants me to have the same exchange. As two energy-metabolizing creatures, we consent to be with each other and feed on the other. Realizing that neither of us are human was interesting, but the mutual consent between us is really important to me.

After Cassandra's birth, he started encouraging me to feed more often, especially with how draining those first few weeks after birth were. When Cassandra would fall asleep, he'd massage me, kiss between my legs, make me come without penetration, and ask me to feed while he did so. While I was healing, I'll admit having a helping of his strength helped.

William and I communicate with each other patiently. He has never kept anything from me, not since the news about my dad. While at times it isn't easy to hear everything he has to say, it's true. Our honesty, passion for each other, our joy to try new experiences...There are so many reasons why we just work. I'm a lucky bride. He helps me see who I am, a kind warrior and not a monster for what I was born into.

And nothing is hotter than my husband's demon dick. As I blink the sleep from my eyes, I find William still asleep and naked beside me. The doors to our room are open to the sea air, but our nakedness doesn't matter. William reserved all the huts within view of ours so we could have the privacy to do whatever we pleased whenever we wanted. Our bungalow room is comfortable with softer sheets and bedding than even the ones we splurged on at home. It makes me never want to leave our bed, and other than when I want to swim, I barely move. In the heat of the Maldives, our windows and doors are always open to the sun and water.

I rise slowly, trying not to wake him. Walking around to his side of the bed, I stand naked beside him and blow air on his body, focusing on his cock. It jumps in his sleep, growing before my eyes. I lick my lips as I watch each part of him swell and the bumpy ridges rise. Bending down, I lick the tip. William awakens with a moan, his cock hard as rock seconds later. I take this as encouragement and fit my mouth as far down on him as I can. He is wide, so I don't make it far. After a few strokes with my mouth, William roars and pulls me off by the hair. He stands, releasing me and capturing my mouth. His tongue swirls with mine as he pinches my hips.

"Do you want to get in the pool?" I ask as I pull back.

"Only if you stay just as you are," he says with a purr, dipping down to kiss my breasts.

I stopped breastfeeding a few months ago and initially felt insecure about my breasts returning to a normal size with some excess skin. William doesn't seem to mind given his constant attention to them.

I jump up and he grips my ass, bracing me while he walks. As we enter the water naked—cold, despite the sun—I shiver in pleasure. The cold will never bother me, not with his lower body temperature and the years where I was used to his presence. The cold is my friend and often a precursor to my pleasure.

He leans my naked body over the side of the pool, my top half spilling over as he angles my pussy to be face level with his mouth. I moan loudly as he licks me, taking his meal. My ass bounces in his face as I push back into his mouth over and over. The crystal clear waters in front of me remind me of how lucky I am to be his angel, his Emily, enjoying such a pleasurable and welcoming life.

I come loudly and he laps up my juices, sticking two fingers in me to egg me on through my bliss. When I've settled, overwhelmed, he slowly pulls the rest of my body back into the cool water and slits me over his cock. I hold onto his neck as he pumps me up and down in the shallow end, making waves across our private pool.

"I'm going to come in you, make you pregnant again, fill your body until you are shaking," he murmurs into my ear. I smile against his neck and shiver contentedly. I would want nothing more.

He continues to make love to me, holding me. Chest to chest we breathe together. I kiss up his neck slowly and he hums. I feel the reverberation in the column of his throat and I lick up the remaining inch to nibble on his earlobe.

"My Emily, my angel..."

"My William, my ghost, my demon," I say back. My hands go up into his wet hair and tug. His lips caress mine and it's my turn to moan. When he releases into me, I climax with him, riding the wave together as the sun kisses our shoulders.

When we settle onto a chaise together in the shade by our pool, I wrap my arms around him and William covers me in the luxurious plush towels. I feel centered and peaceful in a way that I never expected I would have when I first pursued a relationship with the ghost that had haunted me since childhood.

William caresses my back as we lay together and I rest my head in the crook of his arms. I feel William's incubus passion flare between me again after a few short minutes and I laugh jokingly.

"Again?" I ask.

"Always," he replies.

"I don't mind that."

And we went for round three of the day.

Did you enjoy this Creature Craving?

Leave a review of HAUNT and then
continue reading with book two, BLAZE.

<u>On the Cravings Menu:</u>
*Grumpy/Sunshine between an energy vampire (Emily's
sister) and a chaos demon*

Thank you for reading Haunt! Share a photo of the book and your review at one of the book distributors linked below. Reviews help books succeed, thank you for the support!

ACKNOWLEDGMENTS

This book was a dream, literally. After a nap one day, I sprung up with the idea and couldn't put it down. From there, a whole new world opened up for me (both fictionally and socially) and I felt like I had a new creative calling. I'm grateful I listened to that weird nudge and got such a fun book out of it.

If you haven't listened to your intuition lately, be sure to do so. She'll never stray you wrong.

Thank you for reading book one in this new adventure, the Creature Cravings series. I am grateful that I'm not the only one that was compelled to go all-in with ghost smut. Though now that you've read it, I can celebrate with you the hidden incubus and energy vampire plot. Were you surprised? Let me know on Instagram!

Thank you to the Sprint Queens for encouraging me on this writing journey. Thank you to Freedom Editorial for reading and editing my first paranormal smut book. Thank you to my husband for putting up with me when I locked myself away in the dark to write.

But mostly, I want to send a big thank you to myself for not chickening out, going all in, and letting the wild parts free.

Until next time,

Rachel

About the Author

Rachel H. Drake is the sweet and spicy author, where the romance makes you giggle and the spice makes you hot.

Learn more about her books and the Creature Cravings series on rachelhdrake.com

instagram.com/rachelhdrake

tiktok.com/@rachelhdrake

CPSIA information can be obtained
at www.ICGtesting.com
Printed in the USA
BVHW051809301222
655336BV00025B/591